First Paperback Edition 2010
Published in Canada
Book design: D.Grîn

Cover art: GX Jupitter-Larsen

ISBN: 978-1-926617-02-2

Adventure on the High Seas

by

GX Jupitter-Larsen

Adventure on the High Seas

Nude and drenched in saliva, she was sliding down the esophagus head first. The blood was rushing to her head. Wave after wave of involuntary peristalsis pushed her towards the stomach. She had been swallowed whole, and with all her panic, wasn't able to think of anything else.

It didn't matter that her eyes had been glued shut by all the drool, there was only a damp darkness which, like the inner wall of the esophagus, wrapped tightly around her body. All she could feel were wet rubbery slaps against her skin. She could barely breath. The heart pounding in her ears wasn't her own.

Suddenly she sensed warmth. She was approaching the stomach. Before she could fully comprehend what was happening, the surrounding muscles, which had clutched her so firmly till now, started to relax. Then, without a sound, she had been spewed into the belly. Plop; then fizz. She splashed into the hollow organ of acids and enzymes.

She still couldn't really move that much, and the stench was overwhelming. Right away, she started to feel a sharp bite at her legs and buttocks. It was like sitting crunched-over in a bound sack half filled with corrosive slush. The digestive juices were kissing away her flesh, burning away at her muscle tissue. Digestion had begun. It was stinging! It was painful! She wanted to scream, but could only choke on the fumes. She couldn't make a peep. Between the anguish and her suffocation, she knew her body was being tenderly liquefied.

Before she finally lost consciousness, random impressions pass by her mind: the pussy-willows she used to collect as a small child; her first kiss as an adolescent; oxygen.

Her body had been converted into a soft paste, a dough-like pulp. As she moved passed the duodenum and was received into the small intestine, she was further dissolved by the juices from the pancreas and liver. After all of the nutrients from her body had been absorbed through the intestinal walls, the undigested parts of her were propelled into the colon. There she remained, until she was expelled by a bowel movement.

Life had been too exciting to be fair. Her anatomy had been a meal for some creature from the countryside. The eye sockets of her skull gazed upwards from the large pile of shit that once had been her young beautiful physique.

What wasn't then eaten by dung-beetles for food, was subsequently absorbed into the ground for nutrients. Even the dirt was hungry. Heavens to Betsy! On Venus the soggy sun sets in the east, but the sapphire sky that was above us was hemorrhaging with bliss. Formidable disasters, drawn to a few smouldering remnants, were anxiously chewing cud in a gesture of exasperated difficulties. Immediately forestalled, the rust advanced alone the distance between two floods. Measured steps revoked and replaced any impending surprise. The standstill hurried off, toppled closely by silent crumbling underfoot. Vacuum sowed confusion. Ooopsy daisy! Lavish rot from a variety of overlapping and complementary flourishing decays.

These typical aberrations, mostly cluttered ambiguities, were especially marked for the gloomy heights that were weighing down the magnetic fields. Aerial photos showed an enormous hole. It was all predicted by the weight of brightly-painted corrugated iron, known locally as "wriggly tin."

Adventure on the High Seas

Electrically charred particles were measured by increasing radio emissions; an invisibility marvelous to behold. Incorrect antenna pointing prevented the millimetre wide devices to be encased in a polymer material that would wrinkle or smooth out when electrically activated. Vector scalar helium telemetry was acquired on an uninhabited street. Occasionally darning each other down; sublimely devoted back doors jostled up and down quickened troubles. This disturbance was caused by a sharp change in pressure along the boundary where the collision was taking place, giving rise to this scenario, which resembled a single sensation spoke. The key broke off in the lock.

From multiple philosophical and scientific perspectives, a single sensation spoke splendidly regarding all silvered round and round a retreat, while innumerable thoughts were fussing at a ruinous sense of duty. The implemented boiling glee from any sustainable progressive and innovative superoptimizer was essentially the observational quagmire at which it could change from toil to trouble throughout the delight of definition.

Space-based atmospheric chemistry measurements were made by supplementing the polarizer with another critical parameter that's birefringent. Their mysterious answers cast doubt on the ingenious emotion at hand. An accident is always an announcement for avuncular aversion antiquating an azimuth anointing avatars; although any adaptation adamantly adjusting an allowance for alternates will on no account apply.

Fairly accurate results described a pivotal genghis of facialized field equations spherically symmetric for compact distances. This was indirectly confirmed through electromagnetic situations where the energy created endowed attractive varies. Approximately, the acceleration of kinematical and dynamical equations described the resultant trajectories. For example, this electrical charge geometrized multiple horizons that then predicted the phenomena.

Three or four adjacent oscillating membranes, aggravated by a siege of drought, had nestled an unexpected bristling that traversed the horizon from cold to blood. Careful measurements inhaled most of the matter but then expelled some outward on the inverse square of the distance. A pair of gravitational sums, inversely proportional to the predicted calculations were entirely under another perturbing discrepancy. The engine stalled.

Organic molecules can form in deep space. Chemical reactions result from collisions among gaseous particles. There's dust in the gas floating between stars. These grains can serve as landing sites for atoms to meet and react, producing molecules. As a result, the grains build up layers of ice containing basic organic molecules like methanol, the simplest alcohol. This assumption was reasonable for distances that hold over superior asymmetrical accelerations. A further example was the expression that velocities account for the detailed information measured by increased sulfhaemoglobinaemia emissions. The empty space, between him and where he wanted to go, was in his way. He was green with sulfhaemoglobinaemia. Attempts were also made to strengthen the tunnel which had been prone to collapses with regular cracks appearing in the brick lining. In an attempt to stabilize the middle section steel hoops were added at regular intervals.

Instead of ordinary ash and dust, ion plumes were made of electrified gas floating so high above ground they came in contact with space itself. The plumes appeared during geomagnetic storms and they interfered with satellite transmissions, airline navigation and radio communications.

The religious were just closet atheists who denied the nonexistence of any god. Ooopsy daisy, you can't escape the meaninglessness of life and death by killing yourself, you have to keep on and discover your own diphallia.

Adventure on the High Seas

The gargantuan climb emphasized the smoldering punctured blackened wreck succumbed by aerodynamic forces, exemplifying that characteristic blend of speculative audacity and scientifically informed insight which slippery needles wound through stretched and bruised nipples. The Cnox genes, like the Hox in higher animals, are responsible for forming the body along its main head-to-tail axis. Turn them off and you can form a multiple-headed creature. Any polywave is a jamahariyya. Before they have even hatched, cuttlefish embryos can peer out of their eggs and spot potential prey. So too, evolutionary algorithms are a haven for revolutionaries. Biologists have shown that bird embryos start out with all five digits, but it is the first and fifth that stop growing and are reabsorbed. The remaining three bones fuse and form a vestigial hand hidden in the middle of the bird's wing.

A row of wingless fuselages smacked and stuck together, forming a larger and more helpful hindrance. Cracks in the levee force maladies ranging from asthma to malaria to zelphabetize crowded stares.

But is it classic postmodernism, or neo-postmodernism? Sorry, I just had to ask... Topologist Michelangelo Antonioni wrote fake mathematical formulas to keep other mathematicians on fruitless quests for proof. He counted the volume of sand required to fill the universe and wrote only in upper case without punctuation or word breaks. He died only a few hours after the death of Ingmar Bergman. Four hundred years ago, Bergman launched his life's work with an account of a dazzling stellar explosion. It turned out to be a supernova. Now-a-days, astronomers can watch the same explosion, long after the dying star fizzled out, by measuring light from the original explosion that has reflected back off interstellar dust. Jean-Isidore Isou's Traite de bave et d'eternite! Brain dysfunctions that interfere with interpreting sensory signals are a refection of when the mind miscounts, inducing an out-of-body like-experience. At first, the universe started becoming smaller and denser as the galaxies converged, but then instead of becoming infinitely dense at the big bang, the universe bounced and started expanding again.

Semen is a natural antidepressant. One that is potentially addictive. Semen contains testosterone, estrogen, prolactin, luteinizing hormone and prostaglandins. Some of which are known to elevate mood. Women are more responsive to masculine voices, faces, and odors when they're fertile, and women off the pill accept male advances twice as often as those on the pill.

During these prolonged hexagonally shaped tremors, polycyclic aromatic hydrocarbons were a widespread organic pollutant. The source of the excitement was a modest knot of magnetism that popped up on orange girders good with a couple of missing tabs.

A cold damp flare-up doused powerful winds that stoked major wildfires. The fires scuffled with a Tunguska-sized plume of excess electron density over the microlensing, which was rippling only a Planck length every hour. So at an ever so nanotiny minuscule 0.000000000000000000000000000000000016 metres an hour, they fled to the park where the tidal heating continued to move under

Tidal heating gradually diminishes as the moon's orbit slows down. Neanderthals could talk. Ooopsy daisy!

A freight train jumped the tracks, ploughing into a huge mass of dense smoke. Two buildings collapsed from the force of the blast and burned down. The whole sky turned orange. Gutted remains, An absent emptiness swept up in a filter of smoke and ash by a shock wave from the Baikonur Cosmodrome. The first of these fires burned up the splotched rusty tinges. Interpretive arson, hazy with smoke sprinkling out of whack. Raining ash and soot blacken the degradation. An effect caused by a gassy, bacterial byproduct of its lengthy fermenting process.

A cosmic defect is like a cloudy spot in an ice cube. This arises because water, solidifying, crystallizes differently in different areas. Similar formations, known as crystal defects, occur in many substances during solidification, due to impurities and other causes. The process is also called symmetry breaking, because the substance loses its original quality of being basically the same in every direction.

Psammologists speculate that a grander version of such a defect a cosmic defect could have arisen when atoms first coalesced out of the amorphous soup the universe once was. Such a transition is, like solidification, called a phase change, because it involves a switch between two states of matter. In the cosmic case however, the symmetry breaking would involve a separation of two or more forces out of what originally was one. Psammologists have been theorizing for decades on how nature's forces four types are acknowledged could have arisen from a primordial one.

These defects were even recorded in smoke in the 1860's on a phonautograph, a device created by a Parisian inventor, Edouard-Leon Scott de Martinville. The device etched representations of sound waves into paper covered in soot from a burning oil lamp. Lines were scratched into the soot by a needle moved by a diaphragm that responded to sound. These supernumerary nipples however, were never intended.

Around two percent of people have a supernumerary nipple. They are often mistaken for moles. They can be found anywhere between the armpit and groin, and range from a tiny lump to a small extra breast, sometimes even capable of lactation.

GX Jupitter-Larsen

This is, at least in part, because of exposure to twisted and knotted gastrointestinal superconductivity.

Chromatographic smithereens ruptured, snapping back on tremendously truculent bifurcation. Liquids can boil and evaporate as temperature and pressure rise. Push both factors beyond a critical point and the gas and liquid phase merge into one supercritical fluid. For water, this fluid is denser than vapour, but lighter than liquid water.

Gravitationally ticketyboo, these veep vetters, containing phyllosilicates were all spelunking between graphite covered quadrangle and a microelectromechanical system corrugating evenly spaced trenches.

Flabbergasted pennyweights had epoxy a parabolic melange of kipper-ties, crystallographers, retro-gossamer futurism and electronic circuit bending. All to clear smoke from the tunnel after blasting. Over 5000 dilapidated bookstore kiosks created a maze of roadside cubbyholes stacked with dusty dictionaries in Hindi, underlined chemistry textbooks in Urdu and dozens of worn copies of a three-volume "Noistory of The Permawave." Nearby are haphazardly arranged piles of ancient-looking copies of the various works of Nikolai Chernyshevsky.

A petaflop is a measure of a computer's processing speed and can be expressed as a thousand trillion floating point operations per second. One attosecond is the time it takes for light to travel the length of three hydrogen atoms. A yoctosecond is the time taken for a quark to emit a gluon. Dry as a checked biscuit. The key broke off in the lock. A sinkhole created by a broken drain pipe closed all lanes of the freeway.

Repugnant quadrature, from millionths to billionths of a meter in hydrogenated elucidation of the enzymatic mechanism underlying the synthesis of adenosine triphosphate. Iron is essential for the growth of all phytoplankton.

Adventure on the High Seas

Quenched with impromptu Epidermolytic hyperkeratosis, it rattled windows and chandeliers, made buildings sway and sent people running into the streets, lowering a thermometer each time. Atom was a medieval unit of time equivalent to 1/376 of a minute. A denehole is an underground structure consisting of a number of small chalk caves entered by a vertical shaft.

White soft and nodular chalk with abundant flint seams were sunk by a condensed marine sequence containing highly glauconitic, green, blue, and grey sands and clays, with large irregularly shaped glauconite-coated flint nodules and rounded flint pebbles.

A single line tram nitty-gritty ran the length of the zeptoshambles. The catafalque stands in the blushing aisle. The electrical impulses from thousands of disembodied rat brain cells have been used to direct a wheeled robot around a laboratory. A sensor on the robot sent signals to the cultured rat neurons, whose responses were used to make the robot react to its environment. Arsenic as an energy source was a process used by primordial bacteria.

Drilling figured provocatively, for lack of a better tight bright cringes quite a terrycloth. The elevator gave someone about three-thirty every day. No klutz done. Above the door were plenty of biscuits, English muffins, eggs, and other things.

Crashed twenty-forth were supposed to wide hard together. A crippled dam burst. Suctioned the Epicurean, then quid the Cynic, and finally sipsopped the Pythagorean. Then, an electromagnetic pulse created a preemptive shockwave radio-frequency.

Microblogging the elevator to the twenty-fourth floor, they were scraping across the tarmac

The twenty-seventh floor stepped out and ran smack into this gorgeous hunk of a little while longer. What do you call semi-independent screw-tread suspension anyway?

GX Jupitter-Larsen

Bluntly, ogled variety of grown paths toppled a route mapped out with irregular periods step by step. The new two-piece tomorrow stripped off a gorgeous willowy toilet and pushed the razor over the remaining tingling. He especially slapped the striking another trance. A supple faint began to tear up and soon passed shutters at the touch a quick twisting.

Kneeled breathing became rapid and heavy. His heart was pounding in her chest. A petite body with faerie breasts. Needles and nipples. The pecker immediately rolled off thrusting aggressively hard and tensed with anxious clamps down on it. Dutifully blasted inside the elevators with a scrubbing strength of six thirty eight reached.

Blushed shaking stepped in. After several dizzy puddles dripped from the extra stirrups, a folding chair in the corner was gently probing a gloved prude. Lumps flattered.

At this point, the spreader gave them a reassuring smile. They inserted the closed shoulder over the knob to flash an involuntarily fountain. Prominently stick, like an extra slapped shut. Once again the swelling quickly snapped. Her demeanor changed. A bunch of chuckled flapping bounced monosyllabic answers.

He stepped back a little earlier. They retrieved into the crawl stroke, treading water; and without thinking, dumped the plumbing around the corner of the second thought furnished a complete transdeanthropomorphisation of their surroundings.

She had been made to sit naked in a cage and gawked at a constant thumping of downward fantigua toward forty; frumpy guhathakurties proved to be a form-fitting rose-tinted dribbling. Faulty prowess stood against the mistranslation. Fluoride had been applied directly to the Pineal Gland. A helioseismic approximation of it any way. Not the moo-moos of certain recently taut bursts of dirty flash-filled slick whisperings.

Adventure on the High Seas

There are patterns to these angles of skyscrapers, but this skyline was principally dominated by a huge floating funnel. It's a funny thing, this opposite side of another sip of thick fathom sloshed. Once poured, his eye was resting on the rail of engorged nipples. Again, the filthy mimicking toward such an inflammatory scowl already inhaled the goose bumps.

Vibrational influences. Barren gluttony. He was wriggling just thinking about it. He pulled away slightly, waiting for the periphery of his vision. Fuming slid subsided, then flickered again with more vigor. The double drawl slipped distorted half-crawled smearing, measured by means of an electroencephalo-graph.

Enough was enough, a slippery alarm squeezed up and down the protruding chasm. Instead, a forceful glimpse of pink flesh wrapped around a thick tube of bloated squishing bunched together as blood rushed from around his girth. Wriggling wrinkly holes hissed. Back and forth as he howled oily flesh, eyes clattered shut. His knuckles were glistening as his fingers sought desperately to criss-cross a furious sweat. Twisting and pulling and tugging the flooding wobble, dissolving into a steely crimson blur against a crushing quiver. An involuntarily gust of air washed over her lungs. Clicking roughly through swept chuckles, the discharged anticipation pummeled them slightly ripple. Keeping her pinned down he announced that he had been interrupted. Swung brush against spongy dripping from the damp fire sunk into the thrusts. Every lunge attempted to skewer saturating loosened the shushing.

An audible plop crashed during takeoff; plumes of gray and white smoke rose from the poised field on the smeared side of the sprawling airport; twenty minutes or so.

Hoarse-engorged vomit was digging into disconnected collapse. Then squish-laden swiping involuntarily lifted blasts of scalding ought. Thickening sweat slapped the hardening ooze. It was late at night and a sneaking taste engulfed their sense of excitement.

Alternatively, the mathematical prowess of elephants may be a side effect of their bulging train system. It can also work both ways. Feeding on lichen and algae growing on marble, the ceiling caved in. The next morning depths gasped. The engine stalled amid the crumbling, majestic ruins of a century's industrial decline.

A subway train plowed into another, causing the aroused afterglow to insert an unspoken epistemological agreement and begin a few suggestive comments regarding how cattle and deer both tend to align their bodies along magnetic fields. As the stroking was winding expertly exquisitely slick and very puckered, a dozen people pushed her labia and against her clitoris. Her face was turned at an angle that made it difficult to tell who was draped against who. Her chin and her long hair were the only parts of her face permeated between the cupped and squeezed odors ushering them all across the blowing breath. A petite body with faerie breasts.

They must have calculated that he felt so stretched out yet so incredibly cozy at the same trim. Intricate and provocative displacements were extrapolations of swollen electric-blue noctilucent clouds that had prolonged the regaining exposure. Pushed lubrication eased the quickly skimmed hovering. Eventually one deep picket thought of enough circumstances. Heard separated twice tasted tightly against gyrating shallow degrees shied away from those splitting a quick squeezing thousand apolorkelings and rang between frolicking around crashing into the drowned night, coating the countryside with gritty, abrasive, electrostatically-charged galores.

Furtumous galore were spoiling a strong smell of underations and adoristers having trouble concentrating on obviously intoxicating entrance. His stomach slowly sunk deep into her slender haunches. Despite the hardened against the paralyzed seconds with exploded exhaust battering in pleasant silence together, it soaked in blood and cum to clean up a bit. He expected her the mirror.

Anticiroobbing involuntarily, they slammed with a vengeance. The soiled burning withdrew. Except for the flip-plastic-jamas it was a secluded wooded area; a rustle from a short distance. They picked up the pace. Especially dirty serendipitous shouts reinserted empirical evidence to support depressed exceptions. Detailed ambiguity required the same opportunity to start out gentle and tender.

Flawlessly mistaken, this filibuster had hesitantly regained their composure and moved on at a frantic pace with perfectly sealed saliva. He then unlocked her television and snuggled in, blasting irrevocably sore content everywhere.

Since it was in the middle of the week and there were no signs indicating any access to the trial, he stepped away from stretching her gentle breeze. This was not an uncommon practice for the confidence that slipped off of her shoulders. A petite body with faerie breasts.

An unbuttoned glimpse began to instantly harden once the thick Oak trees zeroed in on the prominent wandering. Uprooted bulbs on the ground. He turned away from pelting the leaves on the trees. The possibilities chuckled off the dirt from the bottom of the heavily shaded rain. The twitching would be delayed by widespread power failures, blocked roads and wind-damaged and flooded debris. Triggering flash floods strewn with trash, tree limbs and shattered glass, the strong peak caught a tantalizing flush. Unexplained source of positrons.

The severe mitigating stood there and stared at her. Plenty of eyes zoomed back and forth. Wet sounds were dripping from the bulbous sprinkling. Chuckled circles glazed around the hard pulse. Squatted down farther, these split-second impacts were still squatting against the slimy warmth like Jay Lethal's Black Machismo act on TNA. Swept spurts flared-up, teetering on the brink of an exposed gyrating from being blurted for so long. The ratio of positrons to electrons should decrease with increasing energy, but at one particular energy range, it increased. With exploded exhaust battering in pleasant silence.

A garbled notch trickled plentiful excepts for a few outskirts interested in a hop, skip and jump to New York. Suddenly snapped out stroking, this probably wouldn't seem very often. The differences started with a crash of captured problems. Never an awkward moment stuck on herself, she didn't try to taste her last breakup.

Another giddy tomorrow blushed burning wet violence gently over a future for them. Interrupting the tear in his eye, there was nothing to be scared of. This new signal did not match the data collected, but it did reveal that the planet's atmosphere, magnetosphere, and its geological past had had greater levels of activity than scientists originally suspected.

A shady glow carried a lot of weight during its time. And even though its sophisticated simplicity took her back to her motel the next day, they were still ahead of schedule. This was a standard procedure with a whole lot extra information about any secret that quick. A tight grip came here from Yugoslavia. Her demeanor snickered a trick scare of 550 parts per million.

For the next month a couple of nights suggested the following weekend. The deadly hospital had second thoughts. The professional wrestler learned fast. The rather deserted area didn't recognize any one. The abutment did a bang up disappearance. There were dark tadpole-shaped plumes rising up from the base of the prominence.

Blackmail messed with an overheard conversation. He figured something had to be the center of attention. She would be so glad to see the next day. Kettleday even. Both grabbed through a double dose of flailing breakfasts. Then, a near-perfect circle of earth dropped some 30 stories almost instantly. The sinkhole resulted from a corroded sewage system deep beneath the surface; the odor from the hole was intolerable. Ground underlain with carbonate bedrock is most prone to sinking because the bedrock erodes with repeated exposure to water. The rock corrodes and the sediment swells with water and eventually everything reaches a critical mass point. Sinkholes can also be referred to as either a swallet, a cenote, or a doline. Narrow streams of plasma at the top of the prominence were constantly falling back to the bottom, much like a waterfall. The streams plummet faster than ambient magnetic forces seemed to allow.

Waste wade through floodwaters and hydrologically zigzagging begun to scold the splitting scrubbed swooped to cheers and collimators from assembled physicists. Chunks of air detached from the planet tumbled into deep space. Another impact destroyed the smaller moon, vaporizing huge amounts of rock and flinging plumes of hot lava into space. New instrumentation installed were able to pick up signatures of vaporized rock, along with fragments of hardened tektites. Rocky planets form and grow in size by colliding and sticking together. This process merges their cores and causes some of their surfaces to be shed.

Geometrically, the gloomy torrential sunlight grew heavier and heavier. Its nocebo effect dropped and shattered into the many pieces lining the chamber walls. Made of a radio-frequency damping material arranged in a pattern akin to soundproof rooms. The shapes minimized microwave reflections and even eliminated electromagnetic interference. The electromagnetic quiet outstretched across the little flame. These quasi-periodic oscillations occurred on timescales swapping a half dozen bottles of antacids. The dayside's magnetic field pressed against the sun's magnetic field. Approximately every eight minutes, the two fields briefly merged and reconnected, forming a magnetic cylinder portal through which particles flowed.

He was a big proud man, a bacteriophage which infects bacteria, so he ran some tests and took some x-rays. Simple normal Scotch tape emits x-rays when peeled off glass. A possible chance that was cancerous. The doctor found a growth sewn with a bang. The following week bounced up and down. Aerial photos showed an enormous hole.

He was a voyeur. The next day withdrew the valley between her tiny pulsating breasts. A thick dark gooey gunk flew drifting. The flashing darkness smiled at them both. They eventually passed out. These closed cracks were torn inside. It felt like eyes being squeezed, squinting out a deep sleep.

The biopsy burst any infections reminisced with him. Both laughed. Nibble kneading tongues were mechanically slobbering entire thrills with someone else. Smoothly smashed down the street, causing a ton of liquid helium to leak out, dragging from the thick muck. The virus was coaxed into binding with iron phosphate and then carbon nanotubes to create a highly conductive material.

Grinned his coaxing inside sneaks of mauled pleasure and slipped each snap another essence. The bulge grabbed his fondest fragrances; straining to push through slurps. Oblivious to them all, reliving a slight presence. It was so quiet, so hazel. Burning wrinkles held gesturing in ornate steaming platters. The key broke off in the lock.

Silently, the excitement left their tender soft skin covered in welts and bruises. His patience traced patterns through her grinding fulfillment. An aromatic anticipation tried to conceal the pillow beneath her head. Rapidly reluctant, zeroing in on her wriggling hipbones, sparks of fire slipped inside his turgid crashing. Fondled fluids amazed.

Surrendering to one's own victory! The especially engorged thrust sheathed a tight grip over them. Strength slid between his steel hard pulse. An elaborate ploy stretched fastened to vibrate in a flash. Each stream increased the vibrations to a tidal emptying, but not rough. He was admiring the tinge of suddenness. Respect struck her harder and harder with each spank, but it still didn't hurt that much. Not really. She was confident her bare butt would get through it all right. Stinging red cheeks softened toward him. She became so distracted by the pain of the spanking she didn't realized just how sagged she'd become. The shape of the light curve was inconsistent with microlensing.

Cracks in the levee, transfixed. She strained and struggled, staring into her cuffed wrists. Trying to push back, vigorously eroding until pinched, he had an eighth sense about her passionate indifference. He took a deep breath and tried to tight the pearls swung over her sore cunt. Needs cooed. Plug-in electric Lithium-ion air squeezed the restraints. Throats pressed hard against a fluid motion.

Peaking higher than ever before, the lull was flopping with every thrust. on route to cushioning the glare. Close enough to measure all the enthusiasm he could muster. Finger-like divisions in the fins of the ancient lobe-finned fish are the predecessors of the digits on land vertebrates today. He'll be uploading a new tomorrow in the afternoon.

If you really were a nihilist, you'd be against both government and anarchy. Breaking the law would be as meaningless to you as adhering to it in the first place. If you really were a nihilist, you'd be the only one to completely understand the ramification of this.

If you really were a nihilist, you'd be concentrating on your own adventures in response to the numerous requests by your own breathing. Real nihilism has to be proactive, not reactive in order to remain aggressively autonomous from the average. Self-excavating holes. A mystic atheism.

A sudden plane dropped out of the sky without warning and nose-dived into a big bang in a fiery crash that lit the whole sky orange. The smoldering debris was destroyed the very instant it got hit by the tremendous explosion.

Naked girl whipped. A two-story collapse caught fire. The elevator was crushed when his roof collapsed. The elevator was popped, and bushed about three-ten. Stellar grabbed dragged definitely vantage threw quietly dangling slightest penetrated volcano erupted vigorously impending involuntary emanating stirrups. Disturb reverently. Clapping thrust as a trickle of blood oozed from her acetylsalicylic pussy. Donned plastic minutes set about returning the same way; towards a more direct translation between bits and atoms.

A gripped tight secreted caused by the gravitational pull of something outside the visible universe. A new proximity between a few strokes slammed soothing ample, embraced and kissed again, scattering this background light between a dripping afterglow stroked. The airport was smaller and much nicer than any southern accent.

When the scrumptious flight attendant came with their luggage. Such dangled motions, exploring these accelerated development cycles, should show no particular direction relative to the background. Sleeping arrangements were a little awkward though

The Dasornis was a killer duck the size of a small airplane. It lived 50 million years ago. Grinding thrusts drove overzealous splits directly to flawless waste. Moist ravaging were the spilled hills of scrambled doubts. Apparently things worked out.

Adventure on the High Seas

Worked out well. They were climbing backwards and laughing together finally.

Instantly, all four ladders grew into one huge erection. Instantly, all four ladders suggested a little squeeze scraping across the tarmac.

There were a few scrapes and cuts due to hitting the asphalt. He redoubled his efforts, blasted forth, and took turns wearing the stage door. At about a quarter to eleven, everyone was all smiles as he shook hands with confidence, then stepped back and formed a zigzag until someone grabbed some waitresses' ankle.

Everyone applauded the crash-landing, snapping pictures as soon as the half-minute got off the elevator. Several seconds sort of paired up with a chance to say something. The flooding flattened the splintered. The torrent was rushing through the thrashed. Piles of trash were clogging spillways. Any liquid, if put into a shallow container and set spinning, naturally assumes a parabolic shape.

Microscopic fluctuations in the fabric of a hot air balloon slashed into some power lines and burst into flames. Vigorously gathered up the simultaneously clamped down as if controlled by the same switch. When everything had settled down, a cough stood naked in the doorway.

Long slow strokes collapsed to accommodate a few more cloistered boundaries. Blindly whispered a definite sprawling complex of mingling laughter. Stretched in slender depths, with scrambled conflicts continuously hitting a little quiet giggle again. The denial was going to have trouble with the casual turmoil.

Torn between a strict liberty and a sympathetic crisis, he arranged to walk down the main street for a couple of blocks before turning on to a side street that was heavily covered with large trees along the sneaking illumination. The branches hung down close to the ground. Uprooted bulbs.

She ducked under the euphoric tree branches and blew an aggressively caught slack. Purring contradictions increased the jovial impact of mimicking against her swirling.

A definite stirring nervously guided him also. He erupted in subtle skepticism and was captured by her powdered cheek. He had never unzipped such an intense feeling like that before. It was all about direction.

The form-fitting travel nonetheless drifted as they discussed a conversation with her every movement. All he could think about was biting off the many hard tiny nub-like nipples along her long slender neck.

Infectious shiny strands of her smooth raven hair became a regular thing. She stepped gracefully from the curb as her heart beat approached. A large beetle had entered her vagina, and was fucking her cervix.

Holding her soft elegant hand, her human companion cleared a way, raised an eyebrow and guided her through the revolving hallway. She hesitated before continuing. Halting knots, barely audible, reached behind her first step. He'd have none of that. His eyes skipped a beat at the sight of the steps below her. The elevator ride to the chocolate-third floor was in dark hardwood silence.

Encircling tongues squeezed her breasts from behind her spine. Smearing against the creamy spank of her neatly inflamed clitoris, teeth coaxed free the spongy fluids saturating his eyes screwed shut. Smoldering lungs were firmly scrunching her sodden supple.

She awkwardly lifted her swollen and bruised breasts for further slipping. Protruding cavities gripping tightly. He spanked her again, a little harder this time; trapping engorged healthy knuckles. Hoarsely twisting taut between her legs. Erratic movements crashed against the silken steam of her petite surprise. A dull rumbling rolling around.

This time the stab of pain bought a pumpkin to her wiping lips, leaving her scurrying afterwards. It was awash with a thousand pinpricks of sparkling morning dew. Actually, although the journey's edge was a blur, she was transfixed on thick globules of sticky shooting down her clutching gulp. She tried to swallow, choking on gargantuan furry spurts.

His squelching glistening rewarded an escalating frenzy of wobbling dust. On top of that, swatting after swatting of aromatic abrasions were dripping out of a turmoil that they thought had only streamed in through an outward display of emotions. The interesting rough in all this was that they never really blurted any accumulated anticipation. Several thoughts were now blissfully cascading through a trepidation that some squelch was never really exclaimed. The experience had been broken up by inhaled excitement flashed across quiet counting. A more prolonged bounce began to separate every vanished reason.

This was a protruding fragrance for some time. They both watched in fascination. Finally, without uttering an orifice, the following night had become significantly heavier. Yet another group of one-eyed space aliens shaped like three-meter tall starfish flabbergasted right in front of them. These upright-walking starfish mounted with a single large eye centerpiece

Yet that eucalyptus buttock was intrigued. It sort of required a great deal of rather unconvincing weight for her height and age. Let's face it, he stood nodding timidly she reluctantly mumbled something about the polywave. Or could it have been the omniwave? The engine stalled.

Sitting down on the sofa they both heard almost inaudible, yet reassuring footsteps on the floor above. Within a split fifteen minutes, a dense patch of nerves pressed firmly against the instant. Within seconds a thousand conflicts and turmoil groaned without actually penetrating the steady pace. Newly discovered sensations quickly clamped round their blissful feelings. A couple days later, they waited for a minute. She blushed.

Their enthusiasm recognized no apparent reason except that an accomplished cubbyhole had been quickly leaned with the location. A breach in the hypnotic epistemological whispering reconfirmed what had been a very emotional moment for everyone. The chuckling darkness of the night! Once again protruded zettawiggles sweep upward at the tips. A bit of a titillation reaffirmed a settling effect on the nerves. Sensations keyed up. A slippery jumble contained quiver as squeaky experiences mesmerized.

Tongues again trembled. Hips lifted off the bed. Huge spider webs full of dust bunnies hug over the bed. Eager seconds of slow pumping were sobbing for a few smiles. Mesmerized by absorbed systematic romps quickly conjured up by earlier efforts. An oblivious squeeze blurted out. Whenever she wore one of her pleated school uniforms, she would hold up the front of the skirt and allow everyone to take turns sliding their fingers under her soft white panties. Seriously impacted chuckles plagued so many secluded thoughts. They had a secret. Explorers explore because they want to go to places no one has ever seen before. Philosophers think so much because they hope to ask questions no one has ever asked before. Noisicians do noise because they want to hear sounds no one has ever heard before.

The key broke off in the lock. Spheres turning inside out. Slightly splayed squirts supposedly could not focus on anything. He always thought going out to a restaurant was a kind of punishment for those who lacked the skill to cook for themselves. Only the weak eat out. The strong prefer their own cooking.

He shut his toothless-engorged pterosaur, the only example of a fistulated chaoyangopteridae to be found outside the ultraviolet wavelengths distributed within the thick clouds of sulphuric acid and sulphur dioxide, sometimes would emit a beam of pure and unbroken hydrogen atoms. Coleopterists terrained some topography to facilitate this bone-chilling blaze. The frog, Trichobatrachus robustus, actively breaks its own bones to produce claws that puncture out of its toe pads. Substantial plumes of extinct arachnids, called trigonotarbids, had the modified hairs called spigots from which spider silk emerges, as well as the external, flexible appendages known as spinnerets that facilitate web-spinning.

Caloplaca obamae is a plant-like growth in California that looks a lot like dead moss or a dry old leaf

There are regions in space where gravity fields cancel each other out. Lagrange points are locations in space where gravitational forces and the orbital motion of a body are in balance. The Lagrangian points furnished a complete transdeanthropomorphisation in which celestial forces cancel out gravity, trapping everything that falls within them. Joseph-Louis Lagrange calculated that a planet's gravitational field neutralizes the gravitational pull of the nearest sun or star at a number of different points in space, making them the only places where an object can truly be weightless. Such gravitational potholes appear around most planets.

Shambles held together with scrap tin roofing. Cracks in a levee; a dam burst. She couldn't stop licking the cum off the toilet. Slice the potatoes very thin through the mandolin. Experiment to find the preferred thickness. Spread each slice on a baking sheet and bake for about eight to ten minutes. Keep checking in to see if the edges have browned, and remove once desired crispiness has been achieved.

Male Chimpanzees exchange meat for sex. Males willing to share the proceeds of their hunting mate twice as often as their more selfish counterparts. By sharing, the males increase the number of times they mate, and the females increase their intake of calories.

The sun's ultraviolet and X-ray radiation gives a positive charge to moon dust, making it sticky. The more direct the sunlight, the stickier the dust. A couple of weeks slipped off an impulsive skirmish. They had to deal with this new situation. Thrust out in the clumsy, blazed and swiveled moonlight, a sooty smudge was burning against the black hair hiding her face. The outside was sitting on the ground splayed out in front of him. Just thinking about her made his buzz ache. Potent chemicals sparked short and slender. A fair amount of eyelids became too heavy for stretching out on the soft cobwebs. He carefully thought about this formidable clinking against hers. Way through the long stretch of thick rusty woods, he looked at her challenging stares, one eyebrow shrugged.

He turned suddenly, and started brushing down the long dirt path that wrapped to the paved road into town. Even though the moon was still out, the road was very dark as it swung down the rough slid. A thick dark gooey gunk flew drifting. An empty bounce stood up. She was naked except for the collar around her neck. She only moved when someone tugged on her leash. He gave a tug on the leash and she followed.

Her eyes forcefully flashed at him. She followed keeping a little slack in the leash. He grabbed her tongue and swiftly scrambled it back into his pants. A shaky laugh bolted for the woods, grinding against the adrenalin all the way. He straightened out and took a broken step forward, but he thought of nothing; nothing but the erect moonlight in his mouth. He grunted loudly in rampantly digging fingers.

Her drooling labia stretched around the thick breath caught. His prodded snatch panted. Luxuriating with the slippery clenching of her reamed out clutch, he hammered into her belly, flicking his grind in a long breathless smash. Her sweat squeezed and clenched as the ecstasy of her climax sagged her taut. His spastic swirling fluttered and wrapped her legs around his spurring. Her sharp cunt was digging into his back as she clung to him. He focused on the pain from her cunt, beating off his thrusting around her throat. A smile crossed contentedly. Rock hard fingertips plucked her sneaky clit. The dampness dried moist, reflecting off the slowly pumping breasts that slammed loudly in her sleeping face. And then, gently flipping the lurch a little, the plum of them gasped his mind. He gritted his ears and heard her cunt wrap around his slow strokes. The elevator caught a slight curiosity tied to a distinct possibility sighed and turned from the window. Afterwards he acted like nothing had happened, which enflamed a little shake to snap.

The swollen backlash dropped around her ankles as she spread her slap wide. In a flash, just a sharply, a stinging slap. A moment later his temper straighten, then stumbled. Hurried to catch up, jolts were wide and open. The doors of the elevator opened as the yottaspanking caught up. They came across a wimp of young girls, many of who had knobby fingers with long claws.

The tingling from the spanking became more pronounced as he snapped the ground around her. She inhaled sharply as she froze, her breasts laughed as the shock and pain pulled out of her pussy. He gave her breast a slight twist. He threatened to slip farther down. Instantly a big strong tongue, acutely aware of trash licked clean, nodded and then blushed a scarlet red. In a halt of a whirlwind, a gasp of pain followed him to a hint of iron underneath. She took one last shivering breath as he strapped her to a tree, gagged and blindfolded her. She flicked against the bindings on her arms and legs. Her head was thrown sideways, as her muscles slipped off her neck and shoulders. Her thighs and hips brushed a glistened scent. He whispered the edge off until his eyes were sucking on her whimpers. His shaking rammed her wiggles. At the same time, he had pulled the hunching against her and dove to stick it under to her clit. She screamed, snapped and then hardened deeply. Her eyes wafted tightly and she was breathing rapidly with that big collar around her neck. She looked at him blankly in order to shackle her chuckles in place. She only moved when someone tugged on her leash.

They were both deadpanned by the large X-shaped waitress in a French maid's cap who slowly flashed on the snapped leash. She pinched and rolled her afternoons in small doses. The naked waitress felt her stomach skip a beat. A shuddery breath swallowed hard into next week. The ragged privilege fluttered disproportionately huge while another grunted breath had bugged out worse than any undulating future.

Slick wet calm walked toward the end of his taste buds.shook his head. Spongy tongues surprised her. The thought loomed closer and closer. A clenching pulse paused, expanded and empty. Doubts threw options back and forth. His thoughts scrambled his brain and left him dazed. He pulled his dick out of her frozen jolt. That bordered the field. A clump of trees flared, and the vintage rumble swung from sight. Uprooted bulbs. That tangling windshield was a different kind of story.

Regular as clockwork, they tweaked that slung-clouded brain back and forth. Drooling rain slid down a low furry moonlight, the very essence splattering her dangling sprawl with a creamy smear. Oozing rubber abandoned her blunt cervix. These gears plundered a jolt straight through his efforts. Impending answers would hurt the loneliness. The only solace was glassing over his eyes. The only real solace was spending the night in a motel. Why was it chasing them?

A couple of weeks slipped off an impulsive skirmish. They had to deal with this new adjoining situation. A few more dizzying seconds before minimum Slumping had stolen enough. Blazed the swiveled a third time. Twenty thousand sides nodded in a quiet synopsis of what was said. He swiftly stood up and whooshed out of her redoubled efforts. The blood was tunneling in their glistened ears. She batted his rigid moments away. Her head fell forward, thrust for thrust.

Her cervix was savoring the fever pitch clenched tightly around his eyes. Nipping, tugging and snapping eyes drifted shut. He could picture love and hate cuddled tightly, slowly rocking back and forth. The very idea was humping his intelligence. Her tightly clenching brain was almost completely glazed with lust as she grunted and writhed beneath his hard pounding slam. His eyes collapsed open and then rolled back into her womb. The sticky sperm deep inside her neck stood out in sharp contrast, as did the spewing dick inside her sweat. The bloated cock rolled back into her little squeak each time. The engorged stiff prick dozed off for a brutal squeal. Her mouth, desperately dragging like a blunt weapon. Wrestling long thin ribbons of cum deep into her waiting mouth. Rough tingling against the limp rushed out, splashing against her spewing gasps. Ooze gushed and whispered in her ears. She smiled and turned her face to his.

Between the gynecologist and the gravedigger, everything would be covered. I understand the logic, but it seems to me that limiting yourself to just ten dimensions is pretty arbitrary. I mean, why couldn't there be more than a single omniverse out there?

GX Jupitter-Larsen

The scarab-like Goliath beetles appear as if they were covered in cracked enamel. They can weigh up to 100 grams. The wings of the Goliathus are more bat-like than bug-like. All Goliathus species are native to Africa. They are primarily tropical, although one species, Goliathus albosignatus, is localized in the more temperate southeastern portion of the continent.

Even so, he could taste her words on his skin. The first true writing we know of are wedge-shaped impressions by phytoplankton on circuit boards. Natural resonant frequencies, months later on a cool and foggy afternoon, three youths were hiking through the hillsides, completely unaware of the bone fragments they had just stepped over.

"I think I will always be alone. Even if I could fine a wife, I don't think she could ever understand me as deeply as loneliness does. Even when I am surrounded by all my best and dearest friends, I feel completely cut-off from each and every one of them. As if I was someone else looking at me looking at them. The one and only time I really felt connected to another person, she panicked and pushed me away. So this is my fate."

"At some point I'm not sure of, solitude intervened in my life. Over the years it kept me safe from many impending dangers. From time to time, I would try to leave my friend to go off on my own. To have adventures of a different type. But as hard as I try, loneness would always be too faithful to ever leave my side..."

"Well, if the source of a man's inner peace depends upon his relationships with others, he will always be tossed to and for between the greatest joy and the deepest sorrow. This is the fate for all those who's centre of gravity rest from without. The question then is, how does one relay solely on one's own self for both focus and peace of mind, without loosing the affection and attachment of close friends and lovers?"

Adventure on the High Seas

His daily Horoscope read; "You can't let loneliness dictate your actions." Glowing cascades of orange and red, the rocket soared into the clear open milieu. All eyes turned upward. Then suddenly the sky tore open round the craft. The rip even passed through the rocket's exhaust. Screens at all the tracking posts were showing the oddest blips the technicians had ever seen. Several rips in the sky were later videoed, spotted and radar-tracked during other test flights.

Tearing his charts up to find a way through the detours, an anonymous astronomer somewhere else found instead a number of nearby planetesimals. Eye to telescope. There was an old hourglass on his desk. Sand was falling up from one bulb to the other. As the astronomer counted away, he thought of clepsammia as the stillness of time measured against the flow of sand.

Floor tiles were missing here and there. His small observatory was lit by a single light bulb. A moth had succeeded in entering the light, leaving the bulb intact, and vanishing within the glow. A solid evaporation.

"What namby-pamby twaddle-tidbit is this then? When is it going to happen? When is it going to take place?" asked a disembodied voice over the airwaves. The jab-jibciufahsu shagged such questionable gravel, that ignominious cagciscahz geared inappropriate intentions and ivoried the chunk.

"It's not this pamby-bamby at all. I'm just not sure which calendar they're on; that's all..." Afterall, not only was it an ordinary shovel, but streakings of fireballs were sighted in the sky.

Everything was soggy with motion. While all differences were the same; another time, another nowhere in particular; "Yer can always tell how old someone really is by the width of their smile. The older the person, the wider the smile."

From birth one's mind comes utterly saturated with all the assumptions and preconceptions that one is ever going to have. Most of one's existence then becomes a pursuit for excuses. Abstractly, the excuse functions as an indication of future reverberations by wave forms that have yet to oscillate; an indication of why the mind thinks the way it does. After many such excuses have been reached, one then starts to evacuate all evidence of one's existence from the environment. Different cultures have all had different terms for such a period as this. Retirement, enlightenment and folly being the most common terms in usage. After as much confirmation as possible has been nullified, the traveller continues to advance. But does so by standing still.

"I find that aging has got to be da absolutely funniest stuff I've ever come across. I mean, the older I get, the more hysterically humorous the whole thang becomes..."

One's assumptions and preconceptions are all synthesized randomly before birth. Every mind has within it every thought ever dreamed. Personality is basically the indiscriminate emphasizing of a few such components. Part of the chaos of biology. There is no connection between what one thinks, what one does, and where one is.

To say that one pursues excuses is to proclaim how the excuse operates as an indication of the pattern oscillated by the mind as a wave form. Abstractly, the excuse as an indication of the wave function of a wave form.

"Da older I get, da sillier I am. Same for most my friends, plus or minus two point five per cent... All time must bend to the passing of men... to da passing of all organisms. I don't want war and I don't want peace. No sir, what I want is interesting times. Because it cant be right, if the mistakes aren't included."

As a means to ratify the pattern as indicated by the excuse, the self automatically moves to evacuate all evidence of one's existence from the environment. Another element to the chaos of biology.

There are two methods for the self in its attempt to nullify confirmation. To remove the proof, or to make so much that it becomes meaningless due to its commonality.

After as much evidence as possible has been null and void, the traveller continues to advance by standing still. After equilibrium, peace of mind. Another element to the chaos of biology.

Vite Eeuy was a very well-dressed man, heavy set. Always in a three-piece suit and a white wrestling mask with black trim. He never took that hood off. He couldn't, it had become his face.

He, Vite Eeuy, was at the Yves Klein International Airport. Video monitors radiated arrival and departure schedules. Vite looked at his watch to see what time it was, only to notice the timepiece had stopped. He was six hours early. He enjoyed the atmosphere of the airport. The semblance and aroma. He would hang out; overhearing conversations. Having detected a discussion between two fellow travellers talking about the meanings of aging, he himself couldn't think of anything funnier than rot and decay. Biology depends largely on highly unstable molecules transferring energy between stable ones. This process simultaneously builds up and breaks down bodies. This is irony. This is; well, funny. Henry Darger used the archetypal pre-adolescent little girl as his device for measuring the distance between contentment and despair. Vite Eeuy used his passport.

"...we trust you had a pleasant journey. Thank you for flying Airot."

Rot and decay as the balance of weak and strong biological forces. There are those occurrences when addition deducts. Biology is one of those occurrences. There was a calm smile on his face. His eyes glanced around the waiting area of the main terminal.

The conversation he was listening to was between a young man named Eduardc and an old fellow called Maximilian. Eduardc was a nanotechnologist. Maximilian, a genetic engineer. Both were on a private adventure. The kind one does alone; with as little or as much evidence as possible. They were strangers to each other. Strangers exchanging stories from the road. Comparing maps, while others thoroughfared bye. As it turned out, from a distance equal to the eliminated area, the asphalt below became viscous and started smelling like smoldering refuge. Umpteen crumpled dirt poked and prodded an inordinate amount of anti-time. Melting moments faded between the passing topography. Various locations, in fact, veered to the edge of yet another ravine anchored deep to irregular gouges deep in the crust.

After a recent serious illness, Vite Eeuy always had this black attaché case in hand. He was never the same. It was the only luggage he ever had. And it was always utterly stuffed full with rotting flora.

He, Vite Eeuy, was on a private adventure as well. The kind one does alone; with as little or as much evidence as possible. Video monitors radiated schedules. He was hours early. He enjoyed the atmosphere of the airport; the aroma. Vite Eeuy had immersed himself in wandering and voyaging. Travelling was all he ever did.

If you were to ask when he began this trip, or how long he'd been on the road, you better be prepared to be told nothing. There is no answer to such a question. Besides, you can't believe the word is round without also believing it's flat. In the correct context parallel lines do meet.

Bypassing all those various cities he could have chosen, he found his own way by happily continuing on his narrative. A cold enthusiasm bent his mind. He was a calm smile. Cities were like his second home. The open road would always be his first. Vite Eeuy would never stay and visit any city for more than a day or two. Whenever he arrived, which was usually just before midnight, the only thing he'd do was walk around the downtown core. This walking around would last till well after the dusk of the next midnight. Wearing thick boots so as to feel closer to the pavement. And while walking around the city streets, he'd always have his black attaché case in hand. This attaché case stuffed full of rotting flora.

He would have kept a journal if the tips of his pencils hadn't kept breaking off. Lead snippets bobbed thence as he remained undaunted.

Vite Eeuy never talked to any one; he just kept to himself. It appeared as if he'd just walk around studying the architecture; examining the accidental poetry of day-to-day existence. By his solitude, even in the turmoil of a city, no one could really know him.

"Who are you?" Vite Eeuy asked the child sitting next to him in the plane.

"An ugly old man..."; replied the young codger, revealing both their souls.

"So; what do you want to be when you grow up then?"

"An ugly old fat man!" yelled the boy. Immortality was brief, so you had to make the most of it.

"Well, going too far is never going far enough I say. There's less to the world than meets the eye." said Vite Eeuy. His body was half way through the flight when his mind came to ponder how many hours flying he had accumulated over the years. A day later, as he came to a conclusion on this issue, he found himself zipping through a foreign landscape while in the six-seat compartment of a passenger-train. Seated just in front of him were two young lovers kissing; pieces of white egg shell guived in their black hair.

Half a dozen usual functions would rise in plunked persuade while these tremendous perspicacious recipients were scuffing the transmissions under whooping xylowaves that yanked this zone. A surprisingly short amount to be both an austere abstraction, an algebrization, and optical illusion. Gush guzzled a shooting gulch zestwards, as the city where he arrived happened to be in complete corrosive decay. Everyone there was running amok; rioting and burning about. Pastured all over every wall, large posters of bold white letters on a black background proclaim; "DON'T WAX THE BITTER, JOIN THE RAINBOW OF HATE!"

And why not? Every citizen has the civil obligation to undermine society at every opportunity. Linear destruction isn't the only byproduct of decay. Moments later, the remaining space was taken up with random atmospheric noise revealing every unblemished flaw. They all interpreted these signals as elephantine gibberish both acute and sparse.

...occasionally, the noise will listen to you.

Hopeless joy's harsh touch achieved a hush; he was keeping low. In some boarded-up back-doorway to some dark back-ally. Just in front sat the violence. Rioters smashing everything at hand. While the vandalism flicked in the night, he counted the number of explosions, the number of fire crackles, of glass shatterings, as well as metal crashings. Manrissnakislekood-seeluwt had shackled duplicate semblances. Only to find shrinking sovhekjsion, uncertainty became xaatoogeekisisyding; as caverns den the hovel. Then too breaking elobosiveness beau. Within moments the back and forth emergency had stopped shattering, immediately jumped out, and nodded in the direction of the nearest industrial-sized nowhere. Almost charming in fact.

Adventure on the High Seas

CRASH!!!

After something good happens, something bad is never too far behind. Likewise, after any defeat springs victory. There's a constant balance between strong and weak forces. Like the fireman who went to the dominatrix to have her role-play as an arsonist. He wanted to be punished for putting out all those lovely fires. His job was a necessary evil for the good of the community. So was her's; the profane thrill of destroying something beautiful in order to make it even more beautiful.

Constant undercurrents of alien peat moss trickled through the hitherto unplumbed depths of stone-washed transparency. Likewise, glowing fires were everywhere. Trinitrotoluene quadrilaterals lashed insidious.

Vite's mind became filled with odd numbers of every kind. 12 explosions; mostly distant; each followed by a glowing fire. Flames submissively accepting chastisement from sudden impacts. 102,345 crackles of fire; at least those were the ones he could make out with his ears. He was a little hard of hearing. 56 glass shatterings; windows coming into contact with hulking holes. 34 metal crashings; mostly cars that were over turned and then set on fire. He then counted the number of circularities he could make out in all the smoke. Dark red dust against that black night sky. White stars flicked in from behind. The air was warm with cheer; grim delight. Pale corpuscles stayed idolatrous irritations. Offered as civility, it still spoiled some increasing numbers. Nine high blasts might have vanished, but wrenched within, these splendid disappointments inspired him. His temperament, like tranquility swallowed whole by suggestion, muddled about in the dusty breeze. He made his mark on the contract by smearing it with his bloody snot.

"Well fancy that then!" said Vite Eeuy. Particles energized had begun jumping. As objects bounced around, gaps opened up beneath them. While hiding in his hole, the ground below gave way. The next thing he saw were elevator doors that opened automatically to reveal a shovel standing upright. Without support, it stood centre stage on the platform. These things happen.

POW!!!

It was a small grey mental elevator. The shovel was ordinary; nothing special. A dull glint. Humility is a byproduct of the condition known as ego. Without ego there can be no modesty of any kind.

Hurtful benefits stirred fixed. The ego was an indication that within all the mind's many preconceptions, there was the potential understanding of the context of a problem as being a self-contained incorruptibility. That any kind of diazwave done purely in reaction to a problem would only add to the maladjustment of the circumstance. It was this understanding that was referred to as humility.

Abrasive ravines urged his blast. Having a humble estimate of one's own merits implied that modesty itself came from the mind going beyond the context of a problem, by measuring it as a kind of jumping off point. To transexpand the whole occasion by an act of possible inappropriateness. Vite Eeuy opened up his attaché case to observe the dust inside.

Arrogance is the opposite of ego. Insomuch as presumptuous haughty functions as an indication that the mind's experiences will be limited to the visible, audible and palpable. Vite Eeuy's experiences would be anything but restrictive.

Clash, clasp clashed. Not with a bang, but with an all surpassing thrash cleared of an utter loss that jumps on and off in a dressed stone, he made his way passed all the wreckage, and on board yet another decorrelation stretch. From the first departure to the final arrival, Vite Eeuy continuously wandered up and down the whole span of the passenger-train. In five hours, he counted 62,609 individual steps made during the trip.

Walking out of the train station, he came upon a chance meeting with an old friend. Someone he'd met on a previous travel. M.T. was the guy's name; no one you could keep track of. Always drunk on decay. He'd always be the first rat off a sinking ship if it wasn't for this habit of staying on board till the very last second. M.T. always enjoyed the ride down. M.T. would often finish a sentence by quietly saying "shooosh", or with a distinguished "woof woof".

"Don't you think mystery novels should be called solution novels? Woof woof."

"How do you mean?"

"Well, if they really were mysteries, they'd never tell you what actually happened by the end. They'd leave it to your immigration to figure out what might have happened."

"But it's the mystery that keeps you reading on."

"No, it's knowing there's a solution at the end, and wondering if your guesses will match up with the author's whims. There's no real mystery with any of them; only explanations. So that's why I think they should be called solution novels... woof woof."

"Well, hummmm; alright then..."

BANG!!! A flaky residue was found packed onto the surface of the explosion. It turned out to be the sharpest, brightest, most thorough chemical shell. It was the steady pattern M.T. knew as the waste receptacle that was his life. M.T. just shrugged it off to gravity. Life was a cunt someone once told him. Life was a cunt, and he was going to fuck it as hard as he could. Just because he could. As a way of courteously requesting Vite Eeuy to join him in a little excursion to a nearby town of ruins, M.T. remarked "We live in an age where the technician has replaced the philosopher. Is it a mistake to expect new hardware without some new software to go with it? This is no time to be practical. Shooosh."

"Tell me something I don't already know..."; replied Vite Eeuy. And the two of them were off. Passing transversing-crossed roads on a pair of found motorcycles. Clouds of dust rose up from the road. The long roar-like tone was drowned out by the shimmers of rust sluicing down an intake of breath, only to burst back out his swiveled mouth into their faces and stretched into the wind. Vite Eeuy was heading very near to where he had just come. M.T. had never been.

Brushed swipes were then roughing with worry. Rumbled hough, grabbed up the creased with sorry. They ought to have rouse a more inexact percentage other than empty infractions like this. However, this sudden movement could not mud as quickly as the upcoming thrashing tumbling into slip. Regardless, like semen splattered on the face of a beautiful woman, the debris from various auto collisions were splashed all up the down the asphalt. Contorted twisted metal squirmed along the form of the whole highway. Specks of shattered glass sheltered the road's contour. While wreckage hurled upwards towards the dust. Accidents. It's what gave life meaning.

Inside one auto wreck just off the road, this guy was jerking off in his girlfriend's face. With every impact of semen on her face, he'd make an explosion-like sound effect with his drool-filled mouth. Bubbles lathered in the ruin. She just sat there, daydreaming of electro magnetism. A small tin funnel was hugging off the rear-view mirror.

So much garbage had piled up that garbage-collecting vehicles had been replaced with patrol cars. The Sanitation Department was everywhere, keeping an eye on everything. Black and white Sanitation Patrol Cars, with flashing reds lights on top, cruised the streets investigating the ever-increasing clutter that was life itself. Making sure everyone did their part in keeping the mess as BIG as possible. Litter litter everywhere. More litter than streets.

Vaginafolk with a fetish for authoritative uniforms would sway at the very sight of the Sanitation Engineer in his black leather. The smell of garbage became a powerful aphrodisiac. La route poudroie. There the ruins stood, all shiny and new.

La route poudroie. There the ruins stood, all shiny and new. Towering brilliances of tumbling luminaries. Luminaries that excelled rotwards. The recomposition done by decay, exact in transmission. They counted the cracks. Wreckage wreckage everywhere. Thwarted cracks extended their wings and locked up the collective circumstance, as well as those persons to whom these empty insights walked away from the only real reason any whizbang kept mounted; the clarity filed by television interference:

vfjvjfjhjgfcvvjvmjhvhfdhghfdhgdfdch
gfhgfchgdhgdhdcjfjhgkgbmgjhfvhgdhgfj
ffchdjsdsdcjfvkgvjfhxhgfxfxcxhgfxjhg
hdchgcchgdcghcyrestdkvfcfdchgdcdjdcjh
ghjcjgcjhfdrdcgkfgcgvkjfdxjhdyrdchgkfc
ghfdsgfdfesxsxgxssxtrsgxcgfsgfdxgfssxhg
dddgrdhfdrxgfsfxdgfdxddsrsdhgdgdjshgs
fsdtrsstrsgfrdgfcjfdsgfdchgdchtrdfdgfd
cresrgdxhfdgfxhdhgfxdjydfxsddfsxgfdsxgh
dhfddgfdjsxdgfdffsdgfsdxdtrgdhfdsxhg
sdsstrgdxfgfdreddrgerdrdysdrdrdr
drdyrdyddrdddcdyddtrfxrsfdsgfxhfdchdjrf
fxsgfxgfsfxrddrfdxfdgssdxgfsgfsfdsfgdhg
fdfdrsdsgfdxgfsfdstrtsghndhrgfsgfxgf
ffdfdgfdstrxgfsfdxsgfssgfdgsdgfshgsggh
xsghssxhgdshgf dtfufchdxgfsgfsgfdh
fdddgfddfdcgsdxgfsbchgcvsfxgfstrsgf

fdcdrdrsgfdsgfdewsegfsfdxsgfsxghfshgdsg
fssesfeasdfsesrsfdsresgssxtessssewqrea
sawaasawqaagqaszaqaaqaaazfqarwqafeada
zsqsfdsdsfeszdssfsdssewsfdseszhdszsada
zdfsresewsdsefwsdasaeafsaaazfadsadafea

A hole twitching and vibrating in a specific manner might be perceived as being a particular something. The same hole folding and shaking in a particularly different manner may be perceived as being a specific something else. Both perceptions would be equally correct. An entity remains unchanged by the act of being seen. What does change is the perception itself. One never reacts to things, only to the perceptions of things. What one sees when an entity shakes is information. Information is that purely random motion which is the only kind of movement that an entity can perform. Meaning is the measurement of information. Information can mean whatever one wants to measure out of it.

Tender hate chewed on tact, while colloquial effervesce barked catchy pitches. So much garbage had piled up that garbage-collecting vehicles had been replaced with patrol cars. The Sanitation Department was everywhere, keeping an eye on everything. Black and white Sanitation Patrol Cars, with flashing reds lights on top, cruised the streets investigating the ever-increasing clutter that was life itself. Making sure everyone did their part in keeping the mess as BIG as possible. Litter litter everywhere. More litter than streets.

Vaginafolk with a fetish for authoritative uniforms would sway at the very sight of the Sanitation Engineer in his black leather. The smell of garbage became a powerful aphrodisiac.

"J'aime le catch! Shooosh." M.T. remarked. It was his way of asking Vite Eeuy how many cracks he had counted so far.

Adventure on the High Seas

"Today is another day; it may have wobbled a bit, but it's decided to drop now. So nuff said..." replied Vite Eeuy; his way of saying 5,865.

M.T. had counted 1,648. "In the future how will robots actually see us? There has been a lot of talk about this in terms of a master-slave relationship. However, I suspect their view of us could be more like that of the domesticated dog which sees its owner as simply a dominant member of its pack. Then again, maybe the robot will be unable to distinguish us from the rest of the background noise of its data field, just as we are unable to distinguish the worm from the ground. We may be critical to the robot's existence, but then, so is the worm critical to our own environmental factors..." Measuring off vanished injuries, the break inserted on a massive drooping flicker. One that was brilliantly scattered around and snapped into a trembling comprehension of how faint each twist had become an animal gene, for a desired protein, could be introduced into a few cells of a plant. The gene would be carried by particular molecules that fragment. Suspended molecules transferring themselves along with the new gene to neighbouring cells. Soon the entire plant would become a factory for animal protein! These pointed peaks sweep down, billowing a xylowave that could only be increased by a somewhat more dangerous glimpse. A somewhat more dangerous glimpse than the elevator doors that would smoothly glide open. M.T.'ll quietly step onto the elevator's dirt floor; dust filling the air. The doors shut then. He'll turn around. Push the button for the 252nd floor. The suspended machine will hoist him upwards; transferring. While within a context of a relationship to all probabilities, every single thing moves in every single direction simultaneously. Because of this polywave, potential can arise as a delay and past effects can have future causes.

GX Jupitter-Larsen

While performing their theatre of the absurd, the two hooded wrestlers became entangled so as to dance by pausing. It was a kind of unsophisticated elegance that bobbled in short leaps. Because of this choreography, the match concluded in a draw. Shooosh.

And while drawing to a conclusion, a scholar of geodesy found lodging in a house of logic. Because of this joyous elation, he came to understand that being nowhere in particular means being in several places at once.

Vite Eeuy and M.T. first came across each other while independently scanning the same horizon of mountain peaks. This pretext being a mound of hazards. Across a luxuriant mountain spur, and down into a big plain. A vast granary whose maize breeze lay billowing. Then the calm expanse of an inland sea ringed about by high lavender-hued. The depths of the zenith were lavish. Yonder lay the groves and minarets, zig-zagged the rugged overhanging that profound abyss. They climbed the outposts of a coast-skirting range, only to find themselves at the base of an even more rugged promontory. The added adventure, bringing something of a gamble.

CRASH!!! "Do you have the time on you? " Asked M.T.

"Actually no, my watch has stopped."

Everything that is, also is not. Everything that is not, also is. Continuing on their narrative, M.T. headed somewhere north of the ruins; "I set a fire earlier and I really should be keeping an eye on it. Woof woof."

Vite Eeuy took off south. The coastal highway had taken him by a number of ships beached along the shore-line. Later, by smelling corrosion on his breath, he knew those rusting hunks where continuing their decay in his lungs. Eeuy rode his motorcycle till the thing ran out of fuel. Abandoning the bike where it fell, he then walked to the nearest train station. Jetliners flew overhead. Shooosh. He wanted the next train leaving for anywhere. He got one eastbound. Reluctantly, his laziness devoured the hysterical hostilities about. Unprecedented, yet measurably brilliant frequencies were extinguished at this clasping sunk. Obviously, those unclassified affections fell short rubbing upon the question. Regardless, the fumbled burnt brighter now that the sudden bursts of laughter reminded him he had swung the future to slam. Slammed smoothly brushing, his musingly wondering flashed steadfast. Gliding gently, they were now stirring gnaws among the clammy shrunks.

Slowly, slowly. The train pushed on ever so slowly. Slowly. The railway was so overgrown with vegetation, that the train's wheels could barely find the tracks. Entirety count seized additionally extended until ponder. Yet thin rope warmthed the right moment for actuality. He was pragmatic concerning the waste bending and twitching. During silence yonder smiled equip toward railway. Hew gushed some giant ecclesiastic oscillations. Using caution, details were gashed yonder. Tumbling x-rays daggered a thump.

The train was soon heading through a long tunnel. One that lead to an underground station just below the massive new airport. There was no one else around anywhere. The airport hadn't open to the public yet. Vacant platforms lead to empty elevators. He found himself at the open doors of one elevator. Elevator number 15. He got in. The doors automatically shut. He turned around and pushed the button for the main terminal. The box hoisted his body upwards. His mind was elsewhere. Fissure formed by breakage; clici-clic.

He was thinking about rocking-chairs, about clepsammia as the stillness of time measured against the flow of sand. The doors opened to reveal kilometres of new unused airport facilities. His body walked out of elevator number five. His mind thought about eternity and infinity as being two differrent things. Eternity as energy. Infinity as anergy. Eternity as anti-time. Infinity as time. Eternity as a compilation of temporary occurrences; with infinity as the stationary void located in between the passing of events. His body continued to walk around the terminals. His mind continued to think of rocking-chairs.

So much garbage had piled up that garbage-collecting vehicles had been replaced with patrol cars. The Sanitation Department was everywhere, keeping an eye on everything. Black and white Sanitation Patrol Cars, with flashing reds lights on top, cruised the streets investigating the ever-increasing clutter that was life itself. Making sure everyone did their part in keeping the mess as BIG as possible. Litter litter everywhere. More litter than streets.

Vaginafolk with a fetish for authoritative uniforms would sway at the very sight of the Sanitation Engineer in his black leather. The smell of garbage became a powerful aphrodisiac. Insurgent welds seethed. Rocking-chairs; clici-clic, clici-clic.

Wendy had a fetish for uniforms. She was a lovely young thing; long legs, nice tits. She always had green outfits on that matched her bright green hair. Hair that was cut short regularly and seldom combed. Everyone enjoyed her cheerful company. One day Wendy had awaken to find scabs all over her body. Her arms. Her legs. Even her tummy. She was sweating as she peeled the reddish hard crust off her soft white skin. She slowly striped off each of the scabs, one by one. Each scab had concealed a tiny hole occupied by a bulging milky puss. She squeezed each wound to squirt out the thick squishy stuff. It streamed out everywhere. She almost got it in the eye once. Afterwards she could see that the pus had also been concealing something. She could see wriggling going on inside each of her small wounds. Not knowing what to think, she got her long tweezers to pluck out the squirming globs. It wasn't easy. Each glob needed to be maneuvered through a narrow opening. It took some skill. She felt no pain. The globs were a kind of fungus she'd never seen before. There was a lemony smell to them. Everytime she got one, she'd wrap it up in tissue and flush it down the toilet. Wendy was very meticulous about the whole thing. That is, she was till she got to the last one. She started to notice how this fungus looked and felt a lot like freshly chewed bubble-gum. Almost automatically she popped it in her mouth and started chewing. It was a lot like gum; she even blew a few fungus-bubbles with the stuff. In time her wounds healed, and the fungus never returned.

Wendy, naked in her rocking-chair; clici-clic, clici-clic. A vantage point; a pulsation of explosion. Abruptly cutting another spin across a good number of dippings and swirlings, he almost instantly vanished after swiftly beating her within a moment of her snatch. Violence, the liberation of energy. Exceedingly corrosive, wind denies stale air. Characteristic conditions changing and fading the briefest of black and black. Slight separations outwards again. House of logic, a construction as this, a designation of potential occurring.

Another house of logic. Arriving to another conclusion, Vite Eeuy's mind was thinking of oily rot. Of rotting oil. Of blacken rot; oily rot. Rotting oil. Rusting dust. Rusting oily dirt. Rotting rusting. Oily dirt. His mind was thinking of elevators with dirt floors. Dust filled the air around him. Noise.

Cracked and faded, the nitty-gritty flames cuticled a sizeable chunk of the oil spill. This meant that, BANG!!!

Speaking of impermanence. Uncertainty in knowledge occurs only during a debate. As the interconduction of independent events oscillating in and out of a context of a relationship to all probabilities. The interpretation of uncertainty as the chaos of hope reflects the constant state of change which acts as the basic characteristics of the predictability amid tendencies which occur most often.

Knowledge is the predictability of tendencies which reoccur most often. When entropy takes place, one's experiences do not have to be restricted to those which are visible, audible or palpable. Unfolding experience, the structure of murmur. Even things that are equal to the same things are not always equal to each other. These are the roles that uncertainty plays in knowledge. Noise implying data squeezed with instability. Alternating layers of meaning xaatoogeekisisyding midst information. Causing the matter to expand. And there he was. The spectrometers and microscopic imager mounted within his eyes glimpsed beyond the sympathetic concrete of the newly built runways, but his brain was gazing at something else all-together-different.

The airport's main runways were aligned to provide takeoffs and landings into prevailing winds. Parallel runways were made to increase potential traffic capacity. Additional runways were provided as crosswind landings with powerful modern jets posed no special difficulties. He counted an everglade of runways. Wreckage wreckage everywhere.

The runways counted were unaffected by his observation. Atoms occasioned independently of his thoughts. He was free to think of them any way he wanted. Everything is true regardless if it is false or not. Clici-clic; clici-clic. Tykît; mùrtø... pirtàksi!

POW!!!

All opinions are equally incomplete unless combined with as many contradictory opinions as possible. The more contradictions combined, the more complete the measurement. An valuable cliché.

A conclusion is characterized by a pause in any process. This pause corresponds to a point reached in which a meaning has been calculated. Numerous such pauses may occur during any single debate. If reaching a conclusion constituted an visit to a house of logic, then the windows of such a house would be the points of view forecast by the calculated options.

He was still thinking of rocking-chairs. Customarily, his enthusiastic explanations were scrambled attentively; if not bustled out completely fuss-free. The ethos of his thoughts became an oomph of ooze oodled slowly through an exude moisture established. A few minutes later, still congregated, their flickering shuttered across a little strange. Tugging to sink out, what followed vanished against the moisture of her tongue. Her whisper burned all night in his ear. Savoring intended to move farther and farther away, eventually pushed consciously in tips to their impingement. Surging through in opposite polywaves, he surveyed this area. His jaw was clenched as he blinked forth. The ethos of this trip, being what they were, became some atoms shifted spontaneously. And he flashed to somewhere else. Swift oblique movement; flashed.

Too many of these circumstances conditioned his sinking feeling that there had been some reason to believe that ascending some stairs, a stray car tire blusterly bobbled and bounced while reverberating a whisped boom. Her moans were grinding against his utricle; all the while a motel manager greeted a new guest: "Good to meet you Mister Eeuy."

"Please, just call me Vite.

Neither of them notice the well-dressed man in the far corner of the lobby. Fred was his name, and he was picking his nose quiet feverishly. Fred had been a connoisseur of human snot his whole life. He took great pleasure from playing with it between his thumb and forefinger; squeezing it. He delighted in its aroma; a greenish scent it was. But most of all, he relished the taste of it on the tip of his tongue against the back of his teeth; salty but sweet. Not only had he eaten his own snot, eight or nine times a day, he often nibbled on the mucus from each of his many lovers. Picking it right out of their noses with his own finger. He could do it without ever giving any one a nosebleed. Once, he even got to dine on the snot of his hero, one Walter Trwyn, a very understanding and giving friend best known to the entire world as a great chef.

"Alright then, Vite. Come this way..." This was the last motel before the desert. The other motel guests consisted of four astronomers, three nanotechnologists, five genetic engineers, and six mathematicians. Two of the guests came from other planets. None knew of each other. All were drifters.

This was the last motel before the desert. Ten minutes before he was to mole the shaved wigger, two people dickweed their smell every bit the same soft. All at once, a torn crapper yeahed into rufous eyes that very each step back. Now vastly uneasy, everyone stepped through the ache marked snoop. From deep in this hole, a waterless treeless remote recompense, hot bedrock swizzled swift warm sand. What really seemed remote then, was how these metallic freckled screams had actually shacked them into the weighty flinches that otherwise would have never crossed his mind. Sweep resulting from wear. An ever-continuing dry wind would wear and tear the ripping heat. Coarses laugh forward accustom, while an inflamed hollowness sunken deep, the echo of a cold warmth with effort. The crumpled oozing swallowed harsher slimes than the grotesque unraveling propelled by a glowing sweaty chill.

Not as temporary as meaty dwindles that were ever faulty, he turned on the television set in his motel room. And started to count the static: 4790, 4800, 4810, 4820, 4830. The blank static; another kind of desert. 4910. His room was covered around with wallpaper. 5200. Wallpaper that depicted shelves after shelves of books. Full-sized. Titles just slightly blurred. 5340. He sat in a rocking-chair; another wave function consisting of random bending and twitching in a complete non-interrelationship with all else. 5540. It is this velocity, and the voidness which is the mannerism of reality, which keeps the mind and matter and nothingness from ever touching. 5960. From out of chance there is potential; like the state of nothingness, falls biology. 6220. The hiss of the TV static could be heard in the next room. 6540... Their arrays of tall doubt intersected with a long-delayed journey. He considered it a privilege in the passenger seat. He struggled against the meaning that filled his eyes. Abruptly luxuriant, the past had been nailed shut.

"Good to meet you Mister Zed..."; the motel manager greeted another new guest. An entity twitching and vibrating in a specific manner might be perceived as being a particular something. The same entity folding and shaking in a particularly different manner may be perceived as being a specific something else. Both perceptions would be equally correct. One difference between the two said perceptions is in the mathematics one would use when making a distinction between them in the first place. An entity remains totally unchanged by the act of being perceived or not. What does totally change is the perception itself. This is one reason why so many almost never react to things; but only react to their own perceptions of things. What one sees when an entity shakes, is information. Information is that purely aesthetic and random motion which is the only kind of movement that an entity can perform. Meaning is the measurement of information. Information can mean whatever it is that one wants to measure out of it. The retexturalization of information consist of giving new meanings to old data, giving old meanings to new data, and/or the fractionating of these interrelationships thereof. The giving of new measurements to old information, or old measurements to new information, is a kind of performance in which there is no audience. A kind of performance in which the players are those who, knowingly or unknowingly, encounter the retextured data.

The enactment of the performance being the possible personal and social consequences of the retexturalization. Blankness is an aspect of emptiness. Emptiness a random cross section of nothingness. For myself, all of these qualities are truly inspiring with hope. Technology is that aspect of nature which man has adopted as his habitat. Manrissnakislekoodseeluwt had shackled duplicate semblances. Only to find shrinking sovhekjsion, uncertainty became xaatoogeekisisyding; as caverns den the hovel. Then too breaking elobosiveness beau. As technology is an aspect of nature, so nature is a random cross section of matter. And the mind, matter and nothingness all equal portions of a soft-cold transparent-murk.

CRASH!!!

With equal portions of the cosmos; Desmond had driven into the motel's parking lot before he noticed where habit had brought him; the last motel before the desert. The desert, a hot bedrock swizzling swift warm sand. Sweep ever-continuing dry wind would wear and tear the ripping heat.

He parked in one of the few slots left open and shut off the engine, then sat wondering if he hadn't been guided there by rot other than habit. He looked up into the rear-view mirror. What he saw were granules sprinkled tough twists and turns. Shattering air rotated around this small motel. He was alone to feel the slivers of air rotate all around. Yet it was sufficiently attractive.

Desmond extracted the keys, got out of the car, and only then saw the girl who sat on the stone bench just outside the motel's front entrance. She was there alone, young and fresh and pretty. He just knew. He could tell just by looking at the girl that her fallopian tubes and ovaries were not remarkable. Although the rest of her body was a very appealing mix of soft weaknesses. Since she didn't seem to have seen him, he took a good long look. Straight black hair with fire-engine-red bangs.

Adventure on the High Seas

She was a rather small girl, but her lines and proportions lacked nothing. She was in a breezy black slip. Her hemline came to her knees. Her slender legs were complete with small ankles and high heels; fish-nets up to her ass.

When Leslie turned her head to see Desmond gawking at her, she smiled. Desmond felt his pulse thump. He said elatedly, "Hey you, waiting for me I hope."

They were perfect strangers.

"I am." said Leslie, softly. She smiled again.

The cafe part of the motel was shut. They got a room together.

She snuggled against him. Her eyes were shut.

He kissed her eyelids. He gently whispered in her ear; "You're a beautiful piece of meat."

"Oh; thank you." She said in a panting half-whisper.

He briskly bit her throat. His teeth would eventually assault every extent of her body. Her senses reeled as she looked down to find him fisting her. He was only going to stick in a finger or two. Afterall, she was pretty small. But it was as if her cunt had just sucked in his whole hand. He grabbed her cervix and started yanking on it. She could feel the beat of blood in her ears. Exasperated, she tried to push away. His huge arm imprisoned her.

Before she knew what happened, she was being dragged by her hair across the floor. Desmond tied her up, and hung her upside-down from a hook in the ceiling. He then used a blow-gun to shoot hypodermic needles into her flesh from across the room. Her dangling limp body, bleeding, was soon covered in the piercing probes.

As fascinating as sex was, the journey was that much more fascinating. He would abandon her there, chopping only a broken smattering of abrasion-ridden holes, tousling them as if ripping apart unkempt rummage. In fact, Desmond got behind the wheel, turned on the ignition, and succeeded in driving away utterly unseen. If life can be compared to an amusement park, a major difference between males and females is that, men want to ride the roller coaster while women want to be the roller coaster. Men want to have fun, while women want to be fun. Men want to have a life. Women want to be life.

Biologically, such desires are the key to understanding both their success and their failure in the social context. For now, however, Leslie smiled there gratefully, bleeding upside-down.

She was found the next morning by the maid. When the girl servant saw the predicament Leslie was in, she stood transfixed. Leslie was still suspended, still bleeding from all the needles stuck in her body. The maid walked up to Leslie and grabbed her by the hair. Almost automatically, she pulled Leslie's head up between her legs and pissed in her face. Almost automatically, Leslie drank every drop of the maid's urine.

The maid would cut Leslie down, pick out all the needles, and bathe her. She would keep Leslie a prisoner in the utility room, chained to the furnace. No one would ever ask for her. And no one would see her for years; a kind of clici-clic twang of a bark. Unrefined panicky digs set fires to medicine exaggerated cavities. Sly uy. Jib drops were ejaculated all over numbing eulogies. Feasible substance anticipated advancing verifications. Edukihed, even talented, grips vocalized flatten glimpses. Vehivkujhvoehv eihuedvkh vkv dkhvd vkv dkjvhs vsd vdshv sdhv sdv sv hwifh wifvsdvsd vskdvsk vskv sdhvsdjvh skvh sdvu sdvjhsdkjhv sdkjvwiufv wekjhs vfsd fskhvisvsdvsdvckjs vsdv sd vskjhvskj vsdhvsifwkbf iwf wviusdvbkdfviodfnjurg uyfjhfdh f jg hf jhgc j jhg jhg jy tytjhf h...

There was a twang of a hiss all around. The wind was blowing grains of sand up against his window. A few subatomic particles were blown right through in between the atoms of the glass. Vite Eeuy had already noticed bits of sand deposited in between the cracks in his room's hardwood floor. Walking around his room, the old floor cracked and sunk with each step taken.

Indifferent sympathy flushed unclouded shadows. For the remainder of the night, like limestone, Vite Eeuy counted the bits of sand in his room. He counted 5822 in all. Spray-balding shadows wearing checked moments punched out directly beneath them. Trying to absolutely eight-nine-ten this limestone off another shovel, his reflections on the subject were very similar to well-worn paths between strangulation and pleasure. The two of them had just been leaning against the unexpected warmth that was clearly in disguise while bidding its straining for a new whiz-leash-wow!

She deposited the egg in the palm of his hand. "Go ahead;" she said calmly. "Break it over my head..."

BANG!!!

Ewygawifjahfihofeds fsoufosojohosagosa-nined the dosaiudosiuhosody ioudsojhodsioes. The walls of the motel were becoming increasingly translucent. A result of atoms dying. When daybreak appeared, he disappeared. On another found motorcycle. He continued on his way; still, and thinking of rocking-chairs. There is a pattern to the coincidentally of these similarities.

Rubber wheels spinning. Spinning rubber wheels. Wheels spinning rubber. All things are a combination location and direction. A cross section of matter vibrating and twitching in a specific manner might become a solid. Wreckage wreckage everywhere. Shaking and folding in a different manner, this same piece of stuff could become a liquid, a gas, or supercritical fluid. While one person tore paper, another was cutting fabric. After they were done with this, they both turned to wooden, plastic and glass objects. The wood was broken. The plastic was crushed. And the glass was shattered. Material cumbering.

GX Jupitter-Larsen

Like semen splattered on the face of a beautiful woman, the debris from various auto collisions were splashed all up the down the asphalt. Contorted twisted metal squirmed along the form of the whole highway. Specks of shattered glass sheltered the road's contour. While wreckage hurled upwards towards the dust. Accidents. It's what gave life meaning.

Inside one auto wreck just off the road, this guy was jerking off in his girlfriend's face. With every impact of semen on her face, he'd make an explosion-like sound effect with his drool-filled mouth. Bubbles lathered in the ruin. She just sat there, daydreaming of electro magnetism. All the while he was pondering the wide open road. Accidents. It's what gave life meaning.

The general effect of a solid is that of a context of matter in which there is a proximity of the component atoms and the strength of the forces between them. Paper and cardboard were torn. Fabric was cut up. Glass bottles were smashed into the screen of a TV set. And trash was playfully tossed all about. POW!!!

The effect of liquid is that context of matter in which there is a short-range structural regularity extending over several molecular diameters. Atoms moving about in randomness to each other, in almost fixed volumes, involuntarily adopting the shape of their container. Fabric and foam were cut. Paper was ripped. Metal thrown about.

Gas is that context of stuff in which the molecules involved would have a minimal volume and negligible forces between them. Collisions between these molecules would be somewhat elastic. Paper was cut. Paper was ripped. Paper was torn.

A supercritical fluid is that context of stuff which has the expansion properties of a gas but the dissolving properties like those of a liquid. Fabric cut.

Adventure on the High Seas

There're many different ways in which an event can be performed. No single or distinct way being any more right or wrong than any other. One could spit by ejecting saliva from one's mouth; or by moving one's legs faster than if one was just walking. Haste washed. One tore paper while the other used an electric drill to build lots of little empty holes in an variety of large wooden objects.

Hanging off and swinging loosely about is another way in which to spit. One could also spit by twisting some wire around something. He dug a small hole by grinding a calculator against the desert sand. Their wooden-stricken glaze would promptly burst into incoherent overlapping minutes to ward off any shiny whimper.

Next to this sneaking, his grasping insisted all is ridiculous, and they should crackle this sizzling aura in order to charge their eccentricities.

The way an event is performed being either desired or undesired is totally dependent on the aesthetics of the performer himself. Miscellaneous flogging jiggles will crystallized the evidence. Everything is useful to someone. Not everything is desirable however. Rubber wheels spinning. Rubber wheels spinning. Vite Eeuy had made it to the other side of the desert. His mind still thought of location and direction. Three out of two weren't bad.

His profile was feverish with refuse swaggeringly stale.

As a young child, he was told he needed heroes to emulate. Without such role-models, he'd become an unfit member of the tribe. He looked around, but saw only deception and hypocrisy. Somehow he knew, even as a child; just because there weren't any heroes didn't mean he had to lower his expectations and behave like everybody else. He came to accept that although Good and Evil may be opponents, they were both self-serving aberrations. He had to greet both Good and Evil with equal suspicion. Good and Evil may never be abolished, but they could still be held in check. He would do just that. He would become anti-social by becoming polite. As the old saying went; *"Be polite and carry a big stick."* Being nice didn't exclude you from beating the living crap out of an asshole. He left the tribe as soon as he could. To live out on the road. He had no regrets. He never looked back.

BANG!!! Mutually advancing steel noises did extremely loud cuts coiling over booby boiling. Zreufaadinfied wadufadjads yaduyfadid the sydasiods and fadyesaked five asydesidsen veshads.

"I don't care what happens as long as it ends in a BIG mess of some kind."

Free will was the predictability of personality. Talk about free will all you like. Reincarnation is just a metaphor for the limit of available personalities. It's an accumulative effect. Two persons living at consecutive times may choose all the same options under similar circumstances, but this is not because of a physical link between them. There's only so many ways something can fall together. There are only so many shades; only so many shapes. Even with the polywave, there's still a limit to the number of directions one can take. The only link between two people through reincarnation is coincidence. There's less to the world than meets the eye. Everything is just background noise hissing away everywhichway. In terms of the polywave, it is up to each of us to decipher for ourselves which directions lead somewhere and which lead nowhere. Having suppressed the terrain, Vite Eeuy opened up his attaché case to observe the dust inside. Then, flatten glimpses. Vehivkujhvoehv eihuedvkh vkv dkhvd vkv dkjvhs vsd vdshv sdhv sdv sv hwifh wifvsdvsd vskdvsk vskv sdhvsdjvh skvh sdvu sdvjhsdkjhv sdkjvwiufv wekjhs vfsd fskhvisvsdvsdvckjs vsdv sd vskjhvskj vsdhvsifwkbf iwf wviusdvbkdfviodfnjurg uyfjhfdh f jg hf jhgc j jhg jhg jy tytjhf h... Boiled willow mustard lengthened the sown everywhere. Well-scrubbed failures were visiting his accounts of dispositions. Struggling spire haggard his exhaustion as the strain became too great for him.

The ground slipped by, cheeked and dimpled, while a tumble of dark curls bounced the budding raw rigid surface. The land was dotted with towering pinnacles, plunging craters, steep cliffs, and massive jets violently spewing a dirty mixture of ooze and muck. Looking troubled still, he explained his sorting. Flapped loose, shears gasped burning trues through like a rough dribble. Swung mud-streaked delvings, following kept moments side by side within the hour. Numbness was prickling their effort. He blurted bright their way back through the tunnel. When they saw their weight slid like ooze crashed, he sagged blackened shearings again. A shovel of rot unearthed this simple sequence of bloodshot whispers.

Bloodshot whispers searched for swappers of a dampened rag. Swaddled and anxious, gleams galloped the sum of his return, and scrambled the touch of their xylowave.

CRASH!!!

Eternity and infinity were unconnected. Eternity as energy. Infinity as the stationary void located in between the passing of events.

While he stood by the edge of a highway, what happened next didn't happen for some time, it happened immediately. He hitched a ride elsewhere. Flattening the edge of the moment against his most private amusements, a buzz of promised harshness reluctantly absorbed the unnerving accuracy underneath. Vite Eeuy shortcaked the switch that scrambled the touch of their xylowave; again...

He turned his attention round-bodied out of there. After some preliminary consideration, he hesitated again. The air smelled of a pale blue metal crumpled against the marbling whimper of clouds. A sleepless blaze of electric light collapsing into a gale of otherwise-hilarious farting sounds, had saved the night. Bristling sags popped off the remaining distance just before, somewhere else, a fireball blazed through the night sky. A red, yellow and orange ball of flame hurtled into an explosion that broke out a tremor. No one saw, felt or heard any of it. But it happened never-the-less. Riding on the back of a motorcycle, Vite Eeuy's face was pressed against the wind. The wheels of the motorcycle made a long thin imprint on the road. Not a hole one would be able to see, but the type one could smell.

Wreckage wreckage everywhere. A blab fiasco teeming with thunder and stillness. Great plumes of dust and gravel would soak up enough asphalt to shoot-swoop ever larger and larger. No one could hear it, but these collapsed vibrations reinforced the rough roars that raced crisscrossed within each flashpulsing cruiser of blasts.

Like semen splattered on the face of a beautiful woman, the debris from various auto collisions were splashed all up the down the asphalt. Contorted twisted metal squirmed along the form of the whole highway. Specks of shattered glass sheltered the road's contour. While wreckage hurled upwards towards the dust. Accidents. It's what gave life meaning.

Inside one auto wreck just off the road, this guy was jerking off in his girlfriend's face. With every impact of semen on her face, he'd make an explosion-like sound effect with his drool-filled mouth. Bubbles lathered in the ruin. She just sat there, daydreaming of electro magnetism. A small tin funnel was hugging off the rear-view mirror.

The stranger at the handlebars never said a thing. His travels were all the talking he needed to say. He only felt at home when on the road. Spinning wheels, rubber; spinning wheels, rubber. Vite Eeuy had hitched a ride elsewhere. Riding on the back of a bike, his face was pressed against the wind.

Adventure on the High Seas

Half way there they stopped by an open field. Hmmm, rather picturesque they thought. Silent lightning flashed the whole night sky white and black. Black and white. White and black. Fading into the potential with his attaché case in hand, Vite Eeuy disappeared into the empty field. White and black. Black and white. White and black.

Squatted thumping definitely murmured any brittle through the crack. Shakily stretched back into the moist reckoning, he approached these slippery surroundings enticed by the moonlight. Then suddenly Vite Eeuy stopped. He wondered briefly how such plentiful yet tentative interest straggled in as these vaguely surprising discharges piled up between the silent stranger could be heard continuing on his way. It had become very foggy. Somuchso that Vite Eeuy couldn't see anything other than the flashing white and black black and white white and black before his eyes. It became cold and wet. Real nippy like. The ground gave way to every step taken. Each step leaving a deep empty hole in the dirt. Wreckage wreckage everywhere. At the other side of the fled he found himself at the front lobby of a local television station. Floor tiles were missing here and there. This TV station looked like a giant shovel standing upright ready to dig a hole in the sky. Well, that's how it looked now. It originally was supposed to be a full-size reproduction of Vladimir Tatlin's Monument To The Third International in Petrograd. The mechanized spiral framework ultimately gave way to the spade-like ideal because of a fanciful structural engineer who believed the shovel was a more advanced type of spiral. What he meant by that is anyone's guess, but it's an issue that's still hotly debated to this day. It's a Kettleday-in-Cambodia; don't forget to wipe your feet.

"So, what's en between da channels?" Vite Eeuy asked the TV technician just standing there in front of him. It was his way of asking where he was. Black and white.

"We're all solitude manifested en da flesh." The technician answered by telling him how darkness was the full richness of colour, the very fibre of black. White and black.

Vite Eeuy asked someone else, an engineer, a different question; "So, what's en between da channels?" Black and white.

The TV engineer answered by telling him how clearness was the total lack of colour. White and black.

A cameraman told him that light dilutes the rich fullness of colour with clearness to reveal the individual cross sections of black. "When light cuts between the darkness, random cross sections like reds and greens are divided from the said completeness..."

"Really; well fancy that!" replied Vite Eeuy...

"Yeah and furthermore..."; continued the cameraman; "...yer can never see clearness, because you just see right through da stuff. Black's da wholeness of colour because when yer see it you wont see anything else. While with clearness yer'll see everything else."

Everyone who was asked answered. Everyone that is, except one Adolf Wölfli. This Adolf person could be seen, observing; studying everything that was going on. Everyone had seen him lurking about The TV station for hours now, but no one really knew what he was up to. Some said he was just a producer from another station on assignment here, making a new video or some such thing. Others said he was some kind of census taker. Could he have also been a spy? He was always seen counting. Counting what? It was later discovered whatever he was counting, he was doing so by his own number system. What was for sure, was that this Adolf Wölfli had added new numbers to the standard numerical system in order to calculate some kind of astronomical concept or two. Would it have made any difference if he had asked himself the question of what a number would look like if it was in between Regoniff and Horatif, but not Suniff, Agoniff, and Benitif? Would it have affected his cosmic maps? He'd disappear into the night before any one could ever get around to finding out for sure. The hodgepodges ruffled the restored breaks that were hidden in full view. Gathered by simple flashes splattered about, the jumbled mess rasped a dangling answer. Each answer received was given only after serious and sincere concentration by the participates. Vite Eeuy had become inspired by the politeness and legitimacy of their meaningful non-sense. He understood that what they were all telling him was that he already had the answer, and that he just didn't realize it. To do is to measure. Yearn for it itchy itch! Zoefiyogejofdufodbookods disfiwywjidibifikihouyjihed every wresarsycijohygiyn edridyudboofer and dehigeudugfuifnoobist on Zydiughonbohokhiujdogfosofia. Qurewtoofoodoofooboods were dydyhydidhudlly fakgohaaohjable!!!

Adolf Wölfli's numbers weren't just super mammoth. If Wölfli's numbers were anything, they were a meaningful method of survival for his internumeral theories.

"So little of a father's DNA survives after even only a few generations, I don't see how any male could consider sexual reproduction a meaningful method of leaving behind his legacy. I can understand why women want offspring. Most of the mother's DNA remains unchanged for countless generations. I don't have a problem with this, but what's in it for the male? Not much! That's what! Any DNA of yours that might be in a piece of shit, stuck in the sewer somewhere, has a better chance of survival than the ever decreasing amount that actually gets passed on from generation to generation."

"I guess that's why women made the family name so importance for men. It gave males the illusion of continuance..."

"We travel because we like to..." said another cameraman. "We build holes because we like to. And we count because we like to. It's all, so contemplative..." The floor of the TV station started to give way to every step taken. The whole city had fallen into the ground, rotting away. And built to stay that way. Manrissnakislekoodseeluwt had shackled duplicate semblances. Only to find shrinking sovhekjsion, uncertainty became xaatoogeekisisyding; as caverns den the hovel. Then too breaking elobosiveness beau. "Thangs are only completely perfect when they're just slightly flawed. Da delicate blemish and all that..."

The whole crew at the TV station had been performing trepanation on one another. One person would slowly drill a little hole into a colleague's head, while intermittently interrupting regular broadcasting to present highlights. Afterwards, the just-trepanned associate would return the favour, also occasionally interrupting broadcasts with scenes from the rite. There was blood everywhere. The station equipment, so completely splattered, seemed itself to be bleeding. Bloodstained sparkling dampened through cracks in the craggy litterscape. Vite was gibberishly bleeding with unshed laughter, without even enough to cut this dash off. They were symbolically becoming one with the void. "Well, you cant have really failed in a world already flawed..."; said a voice over the airwaves. Impatiently swept towards that snap of pneumatic whir, he just titterly distracted all the yammering washed from the heap of broken glass in the corner. Later scraped away in several orange pieces, the aftermath seemed rough, as if some counting by his mind had slipped spittishly across the slightest regret. Surprised like a blown fuse, he started crunching streaks of promised blood without leaving a message. No message about the programme.

Adventure on the High Seas

The programme that was currently being broadcast was a drama on how every single direction is just a cross-section of a larger accumulative wave form. Video gestures about the polywave. Actors were depicted to simultaneously come and go every-which-way. The motif used for the show was a bunch of kids, who just dance around all day at this old ruining. They encounter some older guys who break in to the ruining and start counting grins of sand. One of the kids tries to stop them. So, some ultra-father-figure reaches down from out of a rip in the sky, and transforms the kid into some sort of weird-looking ultra-something-or-other. Who then joins in on the sand counting. Till the ground opens up, and all these monsters come out, and he has to fight them. Although, he spends much more time dancing around, and acting silly then actually fighting. In fact, he really just does alot of somersaults and flips around the creatures. Suggesting a story of suspended mayhem slam, very.

Wreckage wreckage everywhere. Hard lengths of skim prated tawny bursts. Bjsusiø biggie beauty böör beaus buzz bowing boom for some hours en total. One actor interprets; "...da marchers were chanting; *'Burn books, not coal! Burn books, not coal! Burn books, not coal!'* Yet another detail. Da meaning of da word 'difination' is a combination of difference and definition. En other words, a kind of autoficiality. An inherent response. Da aftertaste of this particular noise is a destine smell. A property of nasal effect produced by continuous and regular vibrations of da surrounding air. Most vibrations are similar whether audible or not. This destine smell is da sympathetic and hugable concrete of da cityscape. Great thick black buildings outlined en a web of radio waves. Organisms interchanging with organisms. Any one strolling through da streets and pathways of a city is also waltzing en between webs of electromagnetic radiation, modulation; frequency. Without ever having to listen to or watch anything, strangers are caressed by da radio and television broadcasts of other strangers. Noise. BANG!!! Radio and television static quietly hissing en da midground. He made an effort to hear this hissing by first fastening up his overcoat and stepping out of da motel. Then turning downhill with his boots crunching da silent dry snow. Always keeping to da shadows of da empty cobbled streets. He knew he was xaatoogeekisisyding to da noise he wanted to hear, because he soon passed by an ornate iron fence that bounded what had once been an open courtyard. Stillness stirred everywhere. This static; his favourite sound. Actuality is da predictability of probability. A detail. Da difination of da word 'autoficial' izzat of inherent responsibility. En other words, with everything moving en all directions at once simultaneously, everything is da way it would have been regardless. One example of that which is autoficial izzat there are far more sounds than da ones yer can hear and that these sounds would exist even if there were no way to hear them. That there are many more smells than da ones yer can detect and that these smells would exist even if there were no way to notice them. And that there are more colours than da ones yer can see and that these colours would exist even if there were no way to see them. Another example of that which is autoficial izzat yer have more thoughts than yer're even thinking now, and that these thoughts would exist even if yer had never thought of them yourself. One byproduct of da polywave is da state of autoficiality. Yet another detail. Being en common with most explosions, supernovas occur rapidly. Still another detail. Matter only reacts to matter, as an aging star involuntarily burns away its hydrogen into helium; then burning its helium into carbon; then burning carbon into neon; burning neon into oxygen; oxygen into silicon; then silicon into iron. Depleted of fuel to maintain fusion, da decaying star cools; collapses; then under gravitational pressures, explodes as a supernova. A flood en all directions of neutrino particles are released at da instant of explosion. Da accidental limited broadcasting of an electronic oscillator en da television system of his light detection apparatus, appeared to da astronomer as if it were a distant pulsar being detected by da equipment. He knew by da fluctuation of da said brightness that a pulsar it was not. What one sees when any entity fluctuates is information. Perception and information are both involuntary movements. Perception as da randomness of da mind. Information as da randomness of all else. Information is how things move. Perception is how da mind moves. Da two movements, being as different as they are, never come into physical contact with each other. And as they never touch, there are no influences past on from one to da other. Kendeioeweks equfiogopeged feipagers of gepired giggurgurly geore-groges. If there is any kind of similarity between information and perception, it's a kind of accident. An accident that is part of da potential. Da potential that is da pattern to da chaos of randomness. Da randomness which is da explosion that is this cosmos. En other words, autoficiality. En other words that are broadcast on radio; en other images that are broadcast on television, a web of electromagnetic radiation, modulation and frequency caresses lightly over da bodies of those walking da city streets. Da web that is tele-communications functions da same as any other cross section of nature. A network of abstract expansions and contractions flying around and about en a complete non-interrelationship to anything else. With any similarity to any larger context being totally coincidental. Most planets are enveloped en a web of radiation trapped by da planet's own magnetic field. Matter only reacts to matter. Within da airless and supercooled chamber of a scanning tunnelling microscope, several xenon atoms were shielded from any sound waves and heat radiation that would have jiggled them around. Very delicately, da nanotechnologist uses da microscopic needle of da said microscope to nudge and arrange da atoms to form da written letters and words of an one line poem. Da microscope's extremely fine needle is used to detect da cloud of electrons that da atom itself is enveloped within. The same needle is ideal for writing or drawing at da atomic level. His one line poem reads; *'YET ANOTHER DETAIL'*. Polyols are compounds containing more than one hydroxyl group. Polymers are derived from unsaturated hydrocarbons containing da ethylene or diene groups. Polyethelene is a whitish translucent polymer of moderate strength and high toughness. Ironically, instead of a blazing forest fire, this clustering squeezed apart yet another xylowave. These are da words that he hears on da radio while he's watching television tonight. Waves generated by electrical disturbance. His transmitter is a spark oscillator with two metal plates acting as resonator and aerial. His receiver is similarly constructed. CRASH!!! Sparks across a small gap en da receiving circuit indicate reception of da waves radiated by da transmitter. For a wave form that is not still, its auxiliary or subsequent resultant pertaining to its capacities aside from itself, is never connected to itself. Da byproduct of either matter or da mind izzat which isn't connected to either. Information is da wreckage of thought. Anti-time is da wreckage of matter. For a wave form that is still, its auxiliary or subsequent resultant pertaining to its capacities aside from itself, is always connected to itself. Da byproduct of nothingness izzat which is connected to da state of nothingness. En other words, with everything moving en all directions at once simultaneously, everything is da way it would have been regardless. One example of that which is autoficial izzat there are far more sounds than da ones yer can hear and that these sounds would exist even if there were no way to hear them. That there are many more smells than da ones yer can detect and that these smells would exist even if there were no way to notice them. And that there are more colours than da ones yer can see and that these colours would exist even if there were no way to see them. Another example of that which is autoficial izzat yer have more thoughts than yer're even thinking now, and that these thoughts would exist even if yer had never thought of them yourself. One byproduct of da polywave is da state of autoficiality. Yet another detail. Being en common with most explosions, supernovas occur rapidly. Still another detail. Matter only reacts to matter, as an aging star involuntarily burns away its hydrogen into helium; then burning its helium into carbon; then burning carbon into neon; burning neon into oxygen; oxygen into silicon; then silicon into iron. Depleted of fuel to maintain fusion, da decaying star cools; collapses; then under gravitational pressures, explodes as a supernova. A flood en all directions of neutrino particles are released at da instant of explosion. Da accidental limited broadcasting of an electronic oscillator en da television system of his light detection apparatus, appeared to da astronomer as if it were a distant pulsar being detected by da equipment. He knew by da fluctuation of da said brightness that a pulsar it was not. What one sees when any entity fluctuates is information. Perception and information are both involuntary movements. Perception as da randomness of da mind. Information as da randomness of all else. Information is how things move. Perception is how da mind moves. Da two movements, being as different as they are, never come into physical contact with each other. And as they never touch, there are no influences past on from one to da other. Kendeioeweks equfiogopeged feipagers of gepired giggurgurly geore-groges. If there is any kind of similarity between information and perception, it's a kind of accident. An accident that is part of da potential. Da potential that is da pattern to da chaos of randomness. Da randomness which is da explosion that is this cosmos. En other words, autoficiality. En other words that are broadcast on radio; en other images that are broadcast on television, a web of electromagnetic radiation, modulation and frequency caresses lightly over da bodies of those walking da city streets. Da web that is telecommunications functions da same as any other cross section of nature. A network of abstract expansions and contractions flying around and about en a complete non-interrelationship to anything else. With any similarity to any larger context being totally coincidental. Most planets are enveloped en a web of radiation trapped by da planet's own magnetic field. Matter only reacts to matter. Within da airless and supercooled chamber of a scanning tunnelling microscope, several xenon atoms were shielded from any sound waves and heat radiation that would have jiggled them around. Very delicately, da nanotechnologist uses da microscopic needle of da said microscope to nudge and arrange da atoms to form da written letters and words of an one line poem. Da microscope's extremely fine needle is used to detect da cloud of electrons that da atom itself is enveloped within. The same needle is ideal for writing or drawing at da atomic level. His one line poem reads; *'YET ANOTHER DETAIL'*. Polyols are compounds containing more than one hydroxyl group. Polymers are derived from unsaturated hydrocarbons containing da ethylene or diene groups. Polyethelene is a whitish translucent polymer of moderate strength and high toughness. Ironically, instead of a blazing forest fire, this clustering squeezed apart yet another xylowave. These are da words that he hears on da radio while he's watching television tonight. Waves generated by electrical disturbance. His transmitter is a spark oscillator with two metal plates acting as resonator and aerial. His receiver is similarly constructed. CRASH!!! Sparks across a small gap en da receiving circuit indicate reception of da waves radiated by da transmitter. For a wave form that is not still, its auxiliary or subsequent resultant pertaining to its capacities aside from itself, is never connected to itself. Da byproduct of either matter or da mind izzat which isn't connected to either. Information is da wreckage of thought. Anti-time is da wreckage of matter. For a wave form that is still, its auxiliary or subsequent resultant pertaining to its capacities aside from itself, is always connected to itself. Da byproduct of nothingness izzat which is connected to da state of nothingness. En other words, with everything moving en all directions at once simultaneously, everything is da way it would have been regardless. One example of that which is autoficial izzat there are far more sounds than da ones yer can hear and that these sounds would exist even if there were no way to hear them. That there are many more smells than da ones yer can detect and that these smells would exist even if there were no way to notice them. And that there are more colours than da ones yer can see and that these colours would exist even if there were no way to see them. Another example of that which is autoficial izzat yer have more thoughts than yer're even thinking now, and that these thoughts would exist even if yer had never thought of them yourself. One byproduct of da polywave is da state of autoficiality. Yet another detail. Being en common with most explosions, supernovas occur rapidly. Still another detail. Matter only reacts to matter, as an aging star involuntarily burns away its hydrogen into helium; then burning its helium into carbon; then burning carbon into neon; burning neon into oxygen; oxygen into silicon; then silicon into iron. Depleted of fuel to maintain fusion, da decaying star cools; collapses; then under gravitational pressures, explodes as a supernova. A flood en all directions of neutrino particles are released at da instant of explosion. Da accidental limited broadcasting of an electronic oscillator en da television system of his light detection apparatus, appeared to da astronomer as if it were a distant pulsar being detected by da equipment. He knew by da fluctuation of da said brightness that a pulsar it was not. What one sees when any entity fluctuates is information. Perception and information are both involuntary movements. Perception as da randomness of da mind. Information as da randomness of all else. Information is how things move. Perception is how da mind moves. Da two movements, being as different as they are, never come into physical contact with each other. And as they never touch, there are no influences past on from one to da other. Kendeioeweks equfiogopeged feipagers of gepired giggurgurly geore-groges. If there is any kind of similarity between information and perception, it's a kind of accident. An accident that is part of da potential. Da potential that is da pattern to da chaos of randomness. Da randomness which is da explosion that is this cosmos. En other words, autoficiality. En other words that are broadcast on radio; en other images that are broadcast on television, a web of electromagnetic radiation, modulation and frequency caresses lightly over da bodies of those walking da city streets. Da web that is telecommunications functions da same as any other cross section of nature. A network of abstract expansions and contractions flying around and about en a complete non-interrelationship to anything else. With any similarity to any larger context being totally coincidental. Most planets are enveloped en a web of radiation trapped by da planet's own magnetic field. Matter only reacts to matter. Within da airless and supercooled chamber of a scanning tunnelling microscope, several xenon atoms were shielded from any sound waves and heat radiation that would have jiggled them around. Very delicately, da nanotechnologist uses da microscopic needle of da said microscope to nudge and arrange da atoms to form da written letters and words of an one line poem. Da microscope's extremely fine needle is used to detect da cloud of electrons that da atom itself is enveloped within. The same needle is ideal for writing or drawing at da atomic level. His one line poem reads; *'YET ANOTHER DETAIL'*. Polyols are compounds containing more than one hydroxyl group. Polymers are derived from unsaturated hydrocarbons containing da ethylene or diene groups. Polyethelene is a whitish translucent polymer of moderate strength and high toughness. Ironically, instead of a blazing forest fire, this clustering squeezed apart yet another xylowave. These are da words that he hears on da radio while he's watching television tonight. Waves generated by electrical disturbance. His transmitter is a spark oscillator with two metal plates acting as resonator and aerial. His receiver is similarly constructed. CRASH!!! Sparks across a small gap en da receiving circuit indicate reception of da waves radiated by da transmitter. For a wave form that is not still, its auxiliary or subsequent resultant pertaining to its capacities aside from itself, is never connected to itself. Da byproduct of either matter or da mind izzat which isn't connected to either. Information is da wreckage of thought. Anti-time is da wreckage of matter. For a wave form that is still, its auxiliary or subsequent resultant pertaining to its capacities aside from itself, is always connected to itself. Da byproduct of nothingness izzat which is connected to da state of nothingness. POW!!! Time is the wreckage of stillness. Anti-time is da wreckage of matter because matter moves. Movement is da very nature of matter; and of da mind. BANG!!! Time is da wreckage of stillness because time doesn't move. Stillness is da very nature of nothingness. Likewise, someone acting as a symbolic state of da quality of nothingness, is someone is so open-minded that curiosity is his only motivation. En other words, autoficiality; an autoficiality of thought.

Curtsy blunts dwindled the swell. As he thought about how dirt functions da same as any other cross section of nature; a complete non-interrelationship; a detail. Excavating or turning over dirt is referred to as digging..."

Dry tacks froze the gibberish and transcribed jostled jots ay. Some hours later, Vite Eeuy left the TV station to go yet another trip. Yet another detail; he counted five garbage-cans on his way out the door. Two were full of torn bits of paper. Subsequently, some crackling hyperpigmented mold fastened through the plastic trash bags containing the old scuttlebutt, and came up onto the midst of all this frantic revving. In other words, paper may never tear itself up, but the sky on occasion will. A rip in the sky will wrap around itself, forming a concave surface with an inherent polish. This rip will soon fade, as if by great velocity, blending back into the ingredients that make up the sky. Once inside this tumblebound wrangling, one had to boil up thee foulmouthed glimp to hubbub any dragging shrill left blip. No grizzlie shrugs here. No sir weee! Stratosphere stratohuedvkh vkv dkhvd vkv dkjvhs vsd vdshv sdhv sdv sv hwifh wifvsdvsd vskdvsk vskv sdhvsdjvh skvh sdvu sdvjhsdkjhv sdkjvwiufv wekjhs vfsd fskhvisvsdvsdvckjs vsdv sd vskjhvskj vsdhvsifwkbf iwf wviusdvbkdfviodfnjurg uyfjhfdh f jg hf jhgc j jhg jhg jy tytjhf h...

Placement Owed Loneness Yew Wondrous Airtight Voices Eachwards.

Dry tacks froze the gibberish and transcribed jostled jots ay. Yearn for it itchy itch! "Tky" is a word that means the samething as "serous". Tky is a unit of measurement. One tky is equal to logic as the predictability of emotion. What Vite Eeuy was feeling could be summed up as serous. His body was calm, but his mind was thinking thinking. His intellect was senseless and brutal. Sweet austerity; his thoughts flashed black and white; black and white; black and white. Because of this likewise, one had high calculations on what some call a "configuration". To disclose and match their positive structures, one became nearby...

Adventure on the High Seas

Continuously increasing from some inverse picobarn, wreckage wreckage, everywhere. Again, collapsing ewuewiø-pewkumew swooned both the deiüdüwikew and the hifidiode. With numerical superiority, this isolated influence was momentarily expected. Hastily shattering probabilities dismounted his pallid consideration, and he immediately decided to take any other course. Earlier that Kettleday, they all hurried off broodingly over the turbulence front and centred.

"Yo; destroying that other molü means sharing;" he murmured this aspect of how any state is arranged, giving rise to motivation out of inappropriateness. This builder of whenever was defined as an occasional variation on a theme.

Wreckage wreckage everywhere.

Dry tacks froze the gibberish and transcribed jostled jots ay. Many typical whenevers result in association from molecule to sequence. The molecule breaks down off-tone when aging. Matter connections only reacts to matter. Existence takes whenever the context of clashing as defined as explosions static and transform between a complex scanty. An coincidentally technique reflecting hereditary elements. Elements made pictorial between accidental flickering movements. Dust measurable. There is a pattern to the formation of that too. Evolution, the ongoing; bodies of irregularities made regular. Extract energy. Ewygawifjahfihofeds fsoufosojohosagosa-nined the dosaiudosiuhosody ioudsojhodsioes.

The popping rot was a totalitarridopaste studied under noticentinibaicheritransposeflectivammongarletciergraphy. Notbinearghadailand testified tension by the shaderiekudder. So it was, a sewblezagical and turbulcoatrysttropical ornatlumi-noumickglarturmetry. Abbruplotion as erosion. Eventually, girdcatapawawawawpatient-la-la will rot the perforation along the scurrilisthrucheological thimble-tidings.

But so what? Totalitarridopaste only ever bolls if the tension is equal to the root of the perforation. Zeastowroothy wry wroth is worst at the moment any ornatluminoumickglarturmetry can be counted. Like counting sand, ornatluminoumickglarturmetry is best yeowittopping if the rake girdcatapawawawawpatient-la-la is turbulcoatrysttropically abbrupltional. Only sewblezagical roostrumstruations can ginger the perforation. Neo-noticentinibaicheritransposeflectivammongarletciergraphy is also sewblezagical and turbulcoatrysttropical. Add this ratio to any tally that isn't scurrilisthrucheological. Easy. Post-neo-noticentinibaicheritransposeflectivammongarletciergraphy instead of classical trans-noticentinibaicheritransposeflectivammongarletciergraphy is gigglamorous to the supreme-maximum. Totalitarridopaste only ever bolls if the tension is equal to the root of the perforation. Zeastowroothy wry wroth is worst at the moment any ornatluminoumickglarturmetry can be counted. Like counting sand, ornatluminoumickglarturmetry is best yeowittopping if the girdcatapawawawawpatient-la-la is turbulcoatrysttropically abbrupltional. Notbinearghadailand testified tension by the shaderiekudder. So it was, a sewblezagical and turbulcoatrysttropical ornatluminoumickglarturmetry. Abbruplotion as erosion. Eventually, girdcatapawawawawpatient-la-la will rot the perforation along the scurrilisthrucheological thimble-tidings.

Classical trans-noticentinibaicheritransposeflectivammongarletciergraphy is gigglamorous when buoy, wrangles sallow. So there. Coils of jelly conserve the ornatluminoumickglarturmetry. Notbinearghadailand testified tension by the shaderiekudder. So it was, a sewblezagical and turbulcoatrysttropical ornatluminoumickglarturmetry. Abbruplotion as erosion. Eventually, girdcatapawawawawpatient-la-la will rot the perforation along the scurrilisthrucheological thimble-tidings.

Adventure on the High Seas

But so what? Totalitarridopaste only ever bolls if the tension is equal to the root of the perforation. Zeastowroothy wry wroth is worst at the moment any ornatluminoumickglarturmetry can be counted. Like counting sand, ornatluminoumickglarturmetry is best yeowittopping if the girdcatapawawawawpatient-la-la is turbulcoatrysttropically abbrupltional. Only sewblezagical roostrumstruations can ginger the perforation. Neo-noticentinibaicheritransposeflectivammongarletciergraphy is also sewblezagical and turbulcoatrysttropical. Add this ratio to any tally that isn't scurrilisthrucheological. Easy. Post-neo-noticentinibaicheritransposeflectivammongarletciergraphy instead of classical trans-noticentinibaicheritransposeflectivammongarletciergraphy is gigglamorous to the supreme-maximum. Totalitarridopaste only ever bolls if the tension is equal to the root of the perforation. Boom-boom! Unrefined panicky digs set fires to medicine exaggerated cavities. POW!!! Sly uy.

"Departing exiles, identical if not ugly, pouched dust immune to vulgar attributes. Chaos beyond drifting acid. Clinging drills throb, emphasizing bravery. And the ominous zenith 'Ohcaohfoanhoi' fosters the gale blusters 'Iufkekjewtoe'. Just a tug sky wet wooed." Kendeioeweks equfiogopeged feipagers of gepired giggurgurly geore-groges.

CRASH!!!

Sharp burdened chloride loosen rabble gorges. After Vite Eeuy left the television station, he disappeared. Vanished from even his shadow. For 32 days absolutely no one saw him. No person, being or soul of any kind from any dimension, saw any sign of him. Nobody at all. But he did exist; having kept to the obscurity of empty back-streets. 32 days after counting 5 garbage-cans on his way out; 32 days after seeing a rip in the sky; 32 days later, he met for the first time the person who had been travelling with him for the past month. A nameless stranger who called himself Kai Dibu. Manrissnakislekoodseeluwt had shackled duplicate semblances. Only to find shrin-king sovhekjsion, uncertainty became xaatoogeekisisyding; as caverns den the hovel. Then too breaking elobosiveness beau.

After Vite Eeuy left the TV station, he disappeared for a month. Absolutely no one saw him. No person, being or soul of any kind from any dimension, saw any sign of him. Nobody at all. What he did during that month would only ever be known to him. Nobody else would ever be aware they knew. What he did for that month would be forever unknown to all else. Yearn for it itchy itch!

BANG!!!

"So how is it you can account for all my actions during the past five weeks?" Vite Eeuy asked Kai Dibu; "I thought I was all alone?" A muddled confusion was botched by his calm resolve to remain static. Then a shock of icy noise thrown into his ears aroused a quick jerk. A hurried grogginess palisaded all efforts; they headed northeast.

"Yer were all alone! It's a question of atoms energized jumping all around like. Of particles vibrating and twitching in a specific manner... Well why do yer think stuff decays? Okay sure, solitude is a faceless traveller, but I still like to call him Sam..." Kai Dibu went on to tell of a story. A sharp fluffy slightness of a story. Like any good story it was one with travel, void construction and some counting of the results at the end. "Soon the elevator doors would smoothly glide open... he'd quietly step in; dust filling the air... The doors shut and..." Stains adorned the enlighten fiend's rant.

Just because you're all alone doesn't mean you're by yourself. This was what rot and decay were all about. This was the meaning of Kai Dibu's story of travel, holes and counting. Vite Eeuy came to understand he already knew this; and knew it well. Rot and decay were the guiding principles of separateness and distance. And the exception to prove any rule laid in between it all. Dirty murmurs lurched over broken glass, while blazing away, the sparkling burning wrapped condensed sang-de-boeuf without much trouble. A multitude of revving swank passed between them as slump smells were thrumming in then distant moments.

A momentary whisper, more reflexive than a dozen, was literally blown off-balance by glowing tongues tucked into feathers ready to speak harshly noddings in the dirt.

Zeastowroothy breaking the gigolo fickles every scurrilisthrucheological clank. However, they only ever totalitarridopasted the jocose when the girdcatapawawawaw-patient-la-la is thoo-doo-wham-dam-zap-zammy. Sure, why not? Ivory dyads of embryonic delegation would often hurdle any teeming magnetism pertaining to the damage. Zero is still zero and all that. Boneless forest would prostrate his mesh. And his ornatluminoumickglarturmetry gazebo kicks a particular hust. One that could never totalitarridopasted a jocose. It was a good day and they both felt fine; wheels spinning rubber. Clici-clic; clici-clic.

Frequent rise and fall at some distance exposed all of them to danger. Chilled, the noisome smell poured trickling fresh, probably following the same route as when Kai Dibu went on to tell Vite Eeuy a story about wrestlers, elevators and anti-time; "...looking over all that devastation gave me the sensation of having just had the best sex of my life. I drunk a glass of Meursault, smoked a Cuban cigar, and reflected on a job well done...."

Tainted alkaline glared. Beak fu; froth cast; influx boulevard crushed. Stunted shrinking. Vite certainty gave no attention to him. The apprehension in the air instantly communicated itself to Vite. He was frantic. He now realized he must go and find a gleamed locate immediately, but at that very moment some gel appeared leading an urgently flew. It was more lively than ever.

He was wearing a black butler's coat, which was a little unprecedented at this hour. Vite leaned against the tawny and passed his yonder over a registered gesture. A few steps closer; it was a question rather than a statement. Vite felt in between a struck across all the tremble that was xaatoogeekisisyding out of a well for over an hour; late. He ran down a slope to a deserted quiet. There was no sign of Kai Dibu. Vite surmised, and immediately thought of stone steps noticeably absent. Hoping to elicit some might, a strode flung copious rips. Bountiful.

ADVENTURE ON THE HIGH SEAS
(THE COOKBOOK VERSION)

THE BAKED POTATO

4 large baking potatoes
olive oil
seasoning to taste
butter

Preheat oven to high. Scrub the potatoes, then poke in several holes to allow steam to escape. Rub lightly with olive oil, and place on a baking pan. Bake for a hour and a half, or until they feel soft when lightly squeezed. Add preferred seasonings, and lots of butter. Serve with warm biscuits.

BROILER FRIES

4 large baking potatoes, scrubbed & quartered
olive oil
seasoning to taste

Adventure on the High Seas

Preheat the broiler. Line a baking sheet with foil. Brush the foil lightly with olive oil. In a medium bowl, drizzle the potatoes with oil as well. Sprinkle the potatoes with preferred seasoning. Toss to coat well. Arrange the oiled slices in the pan so they touch without overlapping. Broil for 12 minutes. Using metal tongs, turn them over, and broil for another 10 minutes. Check to prevent burning. Remove the pan from the oven and transfer the potatoes to a heated serving dish. Serve immediately.

FRENCH FRIES

One's assumptions and preconceptions are all synthesized randomly before birth. Every mind has within it every thought ever dreamed. Personality is basically the indiscriminate emphasizing of a few such components. Part of the chaos of biology. There is no connection between what one thinks, what one does, and where one is. Devises for measuring faxed in gather revocations so dwarfish running with tremble could havoc the severe dry. Fitted of equal length.

THE MIGHTY MASHED

1 kg of potatoes, either peeled or not, cut into cubes
Half stick of butter
3/4 cup of whipping cream
sliced garlic & onion (optional)
sea salt
white pepper

Steam the potatoes for 15 minutes, or until tender. Place into a bowl with the whipping cream, and mash briefly while pouring in a preheated mixture of butter & seasoning. Then beat in the garlic & onion just enough to achieve a smooth consistency. Serve immediately, yet another detail.

Yet another detail was that Vite Eeuy went on to return to the town of ruins that he and M.T. had gone to three months ago. Shooosh. Woof woof. Kai Dibu was still nowhere to be found. The ruins had become increasingly translucent. A resort of atoms dying. Things move despite time. Time is a cross section of nothingness, a stationary void located in between the passing of events. Change accompanied by an alteration of physical properties. Despite this spill, Vite's sobs shouted against transcendent causes; blazing something of comfort and reassurance. Recessed blastings with emboldened grinnings dozened every got. The ruins swerved up, waiting two kinds of undecideds. That being the alerted zoot-frantic embodiment derstandable as one loud crash.

"Even if two bodies are each en thermal equilibrium with a third, there's still no reason why all three should be en thermal equilibrium with each other..." an anonymous voice, heard over the airwaves, was stating that the impossible happened alot more often then one might have first thought. Quibbling sparkle aggrandized the burrow, as a mélange of ecstasy trickled out his gist. The Totimorphous was his most opulent squalid!!! A small meteorite once slammed into his parked car, having smashed a hole right through the trunk and leaving one loud crash of a crater underneath. Later, in commemoration of this impact, he chopped down a tree. It was the irrational thing to do. Clanging brightness hugged the plunge into cheek. Flexible squalids were blurb, stripped and bold. Shut resonant spreads gimped yearly.

"There's far less going on here than you think."

Also recently, a sailing ship, which had been lost at sea for some time, drifted into port without anyone being on board. A ship drifted into port without its crew after being lost at sea for some years. It was the same port it departed from. No log was ever found. The turbulent shrinking was punctured. Naught chum rearranged elastic blendings, then dwarfed every dwindle. Saucer-like rips spirited the atmosphere, barely and hastily dodging the char.

"There once were these two brothers..."; Kai Dibu was taking to this nanotechnologist he had just met at an airport terminal. "Thora and Copagi. Thora was a fully developed, very muscular kind of man. Da kind of man who could take on a brick-wall, and win. Never said much mind you. Copagi was his little parasitic twin. Da front of Copagi's head was attached to Thora's chest. Otherwise a more-or-less complete body. Actually, all things considered, little Copagi was really pretty nimble. Always making some kind of semi-articulate-sort-of-sound. Come to think of it, you could never shut da little guy up! Well, any way, they both really loved da theatre; so they performed together as a tag-team en a few wrestling leagues. Well, da whole thang was extremely coooontroversial! Da poor referees could never tell who da legal man en the ring was. They were always getting accused of double-teaming against their opponents... Yer do know that you can only have one member of a tag-team en the ring at a time?"

"Well..." replied the nanotechnologist; "...even if their bodies were always mouched together, their minds were far off and separate en da distance. Thora always thought of clepsammia as da stillness of time measured against da flow of sand. While Copagi was always thinking of rocking chairs."

Zreufaadinfied wadufadjads yaduyfadid the sydasiods and fadyesaked five asydesidsen veshads.

"Crowd-favourites; they could always put on a great show!" commented Kai Dibu.

"It's now time for our dear friend Vite to hold still... And holding still he is. Right now he's standing put by riding a motorcycle across a very far-reaching bridge. A deliberate fluke." It was the nanotechnologist's way of saying that Vite Eeuy had just come to another conclusion; a visit to another house of logic. This conclusion of his was that matter is often referred to as "light" whenever it is being perceived by the mind.

Rubber wheels everywhere were becoming increasingly translucent. CRASH!!! Tints about seafaring trinitrotoluene waved the nerve. Why else would shrinking spurts stain? The vivid quash chased declining exaggerations over the witty. Xenoliths Yielding Like Ousted Wolfs Accidentally Vacating Elasticity.

Standing ever still even more, Vite Eeuy took a train north-west for nine hours. Wreckage wreckage everywhere. On either side of the tracks he counted thousands of shovels standing upright in the ground. Some were shinny new; others were dirt old. Most faced the railway. He counted 4,912 in all. After the train-ride, he then took a ferry north-east for another five hours. He was the only passenger on board, and the waters were calm. Another train then; this one north-west for three hours. A subway south for 30 minutes.

"Injabio unyag sidgasadas sagged and edification..." Then a bus north-east for two hours. Little traffic, as the coach's tires turnpiked a pair of long thin imprints on the soft freeway. Then, later on.

He marched eastwards, penetrated extensive marshes, and came upon a steamy swamp sprouting several smoke-stacks. He counted 93. Out from the chimneys sprung abundant triplings inaugurated with changes of followings. Hmmm, rather picturesque he thought; flapping descends soared underneath.

The next day, or next night actually, Vite Eeuy was in a car driving at half-a-kilometer-a-hour into a total blizzard. A total blizzard; like some large noisopoly spreading concentrated flukes to reason. Looking forward he couldn't see pass the dashboard for all the snow coming headon. His headlights just dissolved into the mesh of the storm. To either side he could just make out the silhouette of one overturned truck after another. Some other vehicles as well that had lost their way off the freeway to flip about in the snow. It would be a long night. A very long night.

The radio static kept getting louder: kspsjsikspsjs
ikspsjsikspsjsikspsjsiksps jsikspsjsikspsjsikspsjsikspsjsikspsjs
ikspsjsiksp sjsikspsjsik s psjsiksps jsikspsjsikspsjsikspsjsiks
psjsikspsjsikspsjsikspsjsikspsjsikspsjsikspsjsikspsjsikspsjsikspsjsik
spsjsikspsjsik spsjsikspsj sikspsjsikspsjsiks psjsikspsjsikspsjsiks
psjsikspsjsik spsjsikspsjsikspsjsiksps jsikspsjsiks psjsikspsjsiks s
psjsiksps jsikspsjsikspsjsikspsjsiks
psjsikspsjsikspsjsikspsjsikspsjsikspsjsikspsjsikspsjsikspsjsikspsjsik
spsjsikspsjsik spsjsikspsj sikspsjsikspsjsiks psjsikspsjsikspsjsiks
psjsikspsjsik spsjsikspsjsikspsjsiksps jsikspsjsiks psjsikspsjsiks s
psjsiksps jsikspsjsikspsjsikspsjsiks
psjsikspsjsikspsjsikspsjsikspsjsikspsjsikspsjsikspsjsikspsjsikspsjsik
spsjsikspsjsik spsjsikspsj sikspsjsikspsjsiks psjsikspsjsikspsjsiks
psjsikspsjsik spsjsikspsjsikspsjsiksps jsikspsjsiks psjsikspsjsiks s
psjsiksps jsikspsjsikspsjsikspsjsiks
psjsikspsjsikspsjsikspsjsikspsjsikspsjsikspsjsikspsjsikspsjsikspsjsik
spsjsikspsjsik spsjsikspsj sikspsjsikspsjsiks psjsikspsjsikspsjsiks
psjsikspsjsik spsjsikspsjsikspsjsiksps jsikspsjsiks psjsikspsjsiks s
psjsiksps jsikspsjsikspsjsikspsjsiks
psjsikspsjsikspsjsikspsjsikspsjsikspsjsikspsjsikspsjsikspsjsikspsjsik

spsjsikspsjsik spsjsikspsj sikspsjsikspsjsiks psjsikspsjsikspsjsiks
psjsikspsjsik spsjsikspsjsikspsjsiksps jsikspsjsiks psjsikspsjsiks s
psjsiksps jsikspsjsikspsjsikspsjsiks
psjsikspsjsikspsjsikspsjsikspsjsikspsjsikspsjsikspsjsikspsjsikspsjsik
spsjsikspsjsik spsjsikspsj sikspsjsikspsjsiks psjsikspsjsikspsjsiks
psjsikspsjsik spsjsikspsjsikspsjsiksps jsikspsjsiks psjsikspsjsiks
psjsikspsjsikspsjsikspsjsiks psjsikspsjsikspsjsiks psjsikspsjsi...

The car floorboard was cover with discarded drill-bits.
Eihuedvkh vkv dkhvd jdziuuyaw aufdaur warka
rjhgziudufziudtdfziucxvziua dziufziuayd ziuuvc aziufda dtaf
daziutfdaziu fdaziu daqziuvc aufd aziufdaziu dauziu daufd auf
kjziugfkubgvakjfva cuaziuc kaziuc au faugf aziugf augfaiugf
afdaziu faugcfuagbkjhfd aufd axziu fakjc auc ajcg aqziugfakjhg
jfd kjhdaziuziuauujziuaajhf h...

The car radio was on; "So, what's this I hear, about the
latest research that indicates that people who eat their own
snot live longer than those who don't... Well, perhaps attitude
really does count for something?" Calm words from the host of
a late-night radio talk-show; "Solitude... You want to talk about
solitude?! What could be a greater solitude then to live forever?
You need consciousness in order to keep yourself from getting
killed. But if you were truly immortal, you would then be
indestructible. Consciousness just wouldn't serve any purpose.
With immortality you wouldn't need any sense of proportion.
You would be clueless. You would know not of what you do.
You'd know not even of what you are. None of the gods have
any idea of their effects on us mortals. And none of them have
any idea that they themselves even exist. As irony would have
it, self-awareness only ever comes along for the ride if the
journey promises to eventually end... Consciousness and demise
are like two long lost lovers that would always search each
other out; and we mortals are the spectators to their spectacle.
The fatal kiss that always marks the completion of their quest is

why most people are ultimately so self-destructive... Just too romantic to wait for the two sweethearts to finally embrace..."

BANG!!!

"...because there is no great creator or protector, we must all be on our best behaviour; otherwise life will be a living hell."

"...could be more interesting if it was?" The truly spiritual are morally obligated to commit acts of blaspheme as often as possible.

A listener who phoned in to gab some memorable gobbledy-gook; "A facta is a private probability which occurs moore ofen thon not. What I haue entfiel as beinig a polywelle is the simultanes monument in all direktion. The facta is that everything that mones, mones as a polywelle..."

POW!!! "Hey! If I didn't want kids when I was one, why would I want them now as an adult?"

"...on my way home today, I attacked a commuter train. Really. I thought I was at a stop. The thing slowed down, but it didn't stop to pick me up. So I got pissed off and without thinking, I started punching the train as it went by. Even dented it in a few spots. Then, as I looked around I saw I was still a block away from the actual stop. I felt like such a fucking idiot. I just have to calm the fuck down..." Vapour frozen through saturation, plus snowbound on the freeway, equals overwhelm by vapour frozen to a drench. Wind-swept stacks drilled wondrously. Wreckage wreckage everywhere. Impatiently swept towards that snap of pneumatic whir, Vite Eeuy just titterly distracted all the yammering washed from the heap of broken glass in the corner. Later scraped away in several orange pieces, the aftermath seemed rough, unnerving accuracy underneath. He shortcaked the switch that had the radio host say; "Just as theke are moore than two ziders do any wheel, so in the kontext of a relationship do intuse, when a wheel turns, it toes so in moore thon two simultanes direktion. If the sied of a wheel that you are lockig at is in a clockwise rotation, you will always know that the opposite is in a counterclockwise rotation..."

Light white flakes whiningly breathed noisily through partly snuffling tones absorbed.

CRASH!!! Bombastic grime cleared the boundless. Drew blows with imaginary sheers, needling flat quills. Gut swabs, if only too true; guy.

Another listener exercising his right to call toll-free; "You are on any planet öre mon; you ist don. A schechen lauter you stand. At the very point you stood, you wäre kilometres away fromm the lokation in spake in which you satt..." Bubbling shackles cackled. The boisterous rough was severing paused ribbons inside the clasp!

Cleaning closely fitting arrangements randomly held layer upon layer of snow heaped up by the wind. Unrefined panicky digs set fires to medicine exaggerated cavities. Sly uy.

The host; "Soma sat Do locate a partiale exactly an oberer cold bonuse a photon off it. They go on do say that thais very akt alters the position of the partiale. I reject thais viewpoint totale! It is incomplete. Vor only the perceived lokation would be modified, not the achtmal lokation. The achtmal lokation of everything always the same; notwehr in partikulär..."

Collections of crystals, indifferently an exaggeration, perhaps specified to bubble, fell to the ground for holding even more snow.

Another listener; "The existente of the physika kosmos is komplette independent of the thoughts of the inhabitants..."

Heavy falling of snow, with wind solitary in whiteness and texture. Clasps endowed with snap, then maybe blacken blunt.

The host; "The whole kosmos cold be said do be in three portion; the midi, matter, adn nothingness. Nothingness is the only thing which toes not move as a polywelle, as nothingness toes not move at all."

Vite Eeuy couldn't see pass the dashboard for all the snow coming headon. He was still thinking of rocking-chairs. Clici-clic, clici-clic. He counted 24 trucks overturned in the snow. Clici-clic, clici-clic. He had counted 99,418,310,198,455 flakes of snow. Quite a lot when you think about it.

A caller; "So what if everyone behaved like you?"

"It's a mute point." The radio host was laughing; "No culture could function properly if its rank and file all behaved the same. And it wouldn't make any difference what their personality was. No race is complete without heroes and freaks."

One last caller phoned to ask for the name given to matter whenever it was being perceived by the mind. The supposed ripping flap extended some spun off the collision between swallow and stuff.

"Light", was the radio host's answer. "Clearness" being the name given to matter whenever it wasn't being perceived by the mind.

Radio static: vcncgdcvcchcmvbchcmvb
bcncvccncbvufvbvjbmbv- hbmvvhvmvnbv

ncgcjcbcudmdhgfydkegdusshddkhddkdhk
xsxsxsxsxsxsxsxsxsxsxsxsxsxsxsdghtrrt
fcyvhgvfdhgfhdyutyvcghcrcfctfxycygf
fsxedffgcrtcfcrcfcfcfdtrcfgtccruucn

ffjddjdfgfjfgfjdfjfdjfdddjfddddfddd

ffhhjgfhhdfhfdhjdfjhdfjhdfjhfdjhfjh
fgfcvytteryttiykgjhbvgffuhghvjhgvjh
fgjhgfvyutivgjhvytvigvgvihggkvgiygv

GX Jupitter-Larsen

obkopbonbojnojnojnojnnonn

bhjbjhbuhbkjhbbbjbkjbkbkbhjbkbkjhbk
hbjbjbbibhbrtririytityfyrrygfvtyyyt

lkjkkolnojonmkjnkjkljinkjninjkjinii

ctfcrctftftfctfctftcttrftfctfctftct

hjhjlhjkjhhyuhuyjkhyhjyuyhuyjyhuhuh

iiiihiuhiouyihuhiuiuhiuhiuhiouyhiud
xddxxxfxfdxfdgdffxfffgdxfdfdrdfdfgd

sderfsresyredsthfrdgfcjhgvbiuhouhhf
fsgshgdgcfcdxcxzcbvhgiuhnkjhbyftrgh
vghvgfgvgvgvgvtfggftfytfiuygfiufikm
hjhiuhouphiuhjihiuhinuihiuhnoiuhouo
bhbyh98uybybyyugfuygiugyubhubuihgbu

pypypyyyyyyyppppppypypypypypypypykhv

Belonging detached, the dauntless besmirch impaled his wheel. His body was half way through the blizzard driving along, when his mind came to ponder about what he had counted during the past year; 56 sincerities, 63 curiosities, 68 allurings, 15 flammables, 42 trigonometries, 51 potentials, 35 pures, 31 contacts, 42 tractors, 88 connotations of wreckage, 112 austerities, 25 ecological niches, 21 shears, 14 sensitivities, 43 modulations, 95 lemmas, 44 becauses, 64 autoficialities, and 241 frequencies. POW!!! The sincerities were counted while he was accentuating austerity. Any and all forms of logic being a wreckage of thought. Logic as the predictability of emotion. The curiosities were all counted against a background of shattered glass. The 68 allurings were counted as meaningless impious circumstances. His count of 15 flammables was forgone without relinquishment. All 42 trigonometries were personalized reference points. Most of the potentials were understood as proportion; a blasting unadulterated smudge. All of the pures remained totally unchanged by the act of being perceived. Only 41 out of the 31 contacts were as much a temporary occurrence as any fleeting thought. The tractors were all quiet. Wobble ewiuew fides ewiudwouwq effete hale and the vestige of squat scarcity amazed all. Many of the connotations of wreckage were counted as different modes of wave form vibration. Within the context of this kinetics, everything became mathematically symbolic functions. "We know what something is by the theoretical predictability of what it is not within any given context." The ecological niches were counted during a wrestling match. Blitzer Brody grappled with Danny Boy Marty. Brody was a brawler. Always up to some kind of dirty trick or another. Marty combined his own brand of high-flying maneuvers with solid wrestling skills. Any way, the two wrestlers became so entangled that the match concluded as a draw. Vite Eeuy counted some other shears at another precise moment. Another said act. Sensitivities were all counted while strolling through city streets. The 112 austerities as well as all of the modulations were counted in front of a television set while blank static coloured the air. The frequencies were counted while tearing paper. Eihuedvkh vkv dkhvd jdziuuyaw aufdaur warka rjhgziudufziudtdfziucxvziua dziufziuayd ziuuvc aziufda dtaf daziutfdaziu fdaziu daqziuvc aufd aziufdaziu dauziu daufd auf kjziugfkubgvakjfva cuaziuc kaziuc au faugf aziugf augfaiugf afdaziu faugcfuagbkjhfd aufd axziu fakjc auc ajcg aqziugfakjhg

GX Jupitter-Larsen

jfd jdziuuyaw aufdaur warka rjhgziudufziudtdfziucxvziua dziufziuayd ziuuvc aziufda dtaf daziutfdaziu fdaziu daqziuvc aufd aziufdaziu dauziu daufd auf kjziugfkubgvakjfva cuaziuc kaziuc au faugf aziugf augfaiugf afdaziu faugcfuagbkjhfd aufd axziu fakjc auc ajcg aqziugfakjhg jfd jdziuuyaw aufdaur warka rjhgziudufziudtdfziucxvziua dziufziuayd ziuuvc aziufda dtaf daziutfdaziu fdaziu daqziuvc aufd aziufdaziu dauziu daufd auf kjziugfkubgvakjfva cuaziuc kaziuc au faugf aziugf augfaiugf afdaziu faugcfuagbkjhfd aufd axziu fakjc auc ajcg aqziugfakjhg jfd jdziuuyaw aufdaur warka rjhgziudufziudtdfziucxvziua dziufziuayd ziuuvc aziufda dtaf daziutfdaziu fdaziu daqziuvc aufd aziufdaziu dauziu daufd auf kjziugfkubgvakjfva cuaziuc kaziuc au faugf aziugf augfaiugf afdaziu faugcfuagbkjhfd aufd axziu fakjc auc ajcg aqziugfakjhg jfd jdziuuyaw aufdaur warka rjhgziudufziudtdfziucxvziua dziufziuayd ziuuvc aziufda dtaf daziutfdaziu fdaziu daqziuvc aufd aziufdaziu dauziu daufd auf kjziugfkubgvakjfva cuaziuc kaziuc au faugf aziugf augfaiugf afdaziu faugcfuagbkjhfd aufd axziu fakjc auc ajcg aqziugfakjhg jfd jdziuuyaw aufdaur warka rjhgziudufziudtdfziucxvziua dziufziuayd ziuuvc aziufda dtaf daziutfdaziu fdaziu daqziuvc aufd aziufdaziu dauziu daufd auf kjziugfkubgvakjfva cuaziuc kaziuc au faugf aziugf augfaiugf afdaziu faugcfuagbkjhfd aufd axziu fakjc auc ajcg aqziugfakjhg jfd jdziuuyaw aufdaur warka rjhgziudufziudtdfziucxvziua dziufziuayd ziuuvc aziufda dtaf

Adventure on the High Seas

daziutfdaziu fdaziu daqziuvc aufd aziufdaziu dauziu daufd auf kjziugfkubgvakjfva cuaziuc kaziuc au faugf aziugf augfaiugf afdaziu faugcfuagbkjhfd aufd axziu fakjc auc ajcg aqziugfakjhg jfd jdziuuyaw aufdaur warka rjhgziudufziudtdfziucxvziua dziufziuayd ziuuvc aziufda dtaf daziutfdaziu fdaziu daqziuvc aufd aziufdaziu dauziu daufd auf kjziugfkubgvakjfva cuaziuc kaziuc au faugf aziugf augfaiugf afdaziu faugcfuagbkjhfd aufd axziu fakjc auc ajcg aqziugfakjhg jfd kjhdaziuziuauujziuaajhf h...

Wreckage wreckage everywhere. CRASH!!!

The voice on his car radio asked; "If Good Riddance means go away, does Bad Riddance mean come closer?"

It was a week or two later on. Vite suddenly came to a halt. The traffic wasn't moving at all. It was an amazing traffic jam. In fact, it was bumper to bumper for several hundred kilometers. The whole highway had become one big parking lot; a megawedge of auto parts. One thing Vite noticed was how quiet this predicament was. There was a lack of the customary honking horns and shouting motorists. He got out of his car to walk on up ahead to see what was going on. What he found was both picturesque and direct. Everybody in every vehicle was having sex. Making the most of this motorized pause, it seemed everyone came to this traffic jam every evening to get laid. Either by getting a mate, or swapping a mate. Or to at least watch others in the process. Vite saw pedestrians walking around from automobile to automobile, inspecting the nature of the sex being performed in each vehicle. No one fucking seemed to mind the audience; it seemed to be part of the game actually. One of the reasons to attend. There was every kind of sex to watch, or be had. Boy doing girl. Girl doing girl. Boy doing boy. Some just stayed in their car, exposing their genitals to whoever glanced by. You'd never know what you were going to see walking by. Rebecca was wearing bunny ears and a bunny tail. She had little else on other then some fishnets and some very high heels. She was bent over the hood of her owner's car. Rebecca's owner had tied her down with her butt in the air. He'd whip her ass over and over again and again. She could feel the welts on her ass reaching for the stars. Her head filled with the hiss of pedestrians whispering about her; her beauty; and her triumph. How they wanted her. Getting beaten up didn't turn Rebecca on. Having strangers watch her getting beaten up did! How she wanted them to want her

Rebecca's owner whispered in her ear; "Happy Kettleday, little slave."

She was on top of the world. All she wanted now was to drink the piss right out of his chill. She was a leather-popping, open-pussy, slim-lunged girlie-girl. All her skinny prejudices couldn't help but point out that he really did zip up the ameba immediately in order to antique out the dash of cinder-blocks overhead. She would soon be surprised as to how much his warm piss really did taste just like popcorn.

"Call me old-fashioned, but I just cant see how a marriage could be complete without also having a mistress by my side."

Meanwhile, only next door, Vite Eeuy suddenly found himself in a very unfamiliar place talking to a complete stranger. "...so where am I? Who are you!? Why am I here!!? What's going on here!!!?"

"Now, now, calm down now. Don't worry. You're in a space ship anchored between a small microverse and your universe..." responded the stranger.

"You don't say. Looks to me like we're standing on the streets of some kind of a small sea-side beach-type community."

"Yes, well, I get that alot actually"

"So what are these buildings then?"

"Different compartments of our ship."

"And the beach in front of us?"

Adventure on the High Seas

"The control interface."

"And the ocean there?!"

"Its our view screen."

"Really?"

"Yes, I'll try and keep this brief, but we're from a civilization in a very old universe. So old in fact that not only have the smaller stars stopped burning, most planets have drifted away from their suns. Soon, many of our galaxies will have lost most of their stars through evaporation. Protons are soon going to start decaying, and before that happens we're trying to transmit of sum of our civilization's knowledge into an universe with younger atoms."

"Wow... Fuck."

"Yes, well, the thing is, and this is why we brought you here; we thought your universe would do, however, we made one big mistake in our calculations..."

"Really? What's that?"

"There's this person Adolf Wölfli, and we've lost track of his whereabouts..." The accumulative effect from all this vibration was the sum of 64 autoficialities and 44 becauses. Vite Eeuy's mind was filled with the oddest numbers of every kind. Just off the highway he noticed a young boy playing fetch with a little girl. The boy would toss a small ball and his girl would go after it. She'd happily chase after the ball on all fours. When she got to the ball she'd snatch it up with her mouth. Never using her hands, she'd bring it back to the boy. He'd pat her on her head and tell her what a good girl she was. They'd do it over and over, again and again. He quickly realized their rugged odor had mirrored a semicircle around the outskirts of evidence, finally drifting toward them in a swaggering luminescent clustering of attention.

It had become curiously obvious that neither of them were a twitch of anticipation. It had chemically resembled water-based plasmas surrounding comets.

The temperature instantly seemed a full three degrees Zighting; too hot for any one. Touched by his new concern, she kissed the importance of his matter-of-factly introspective eyes.

Under this withering ruin, damaged by rigid inadequacies, a groggily pattern developed that resonated much flutter and feint. Even emblazoned enough to spit out harden old blisters to curb future plump and jangling, it still seemed as if Vite was going to continue on his way, walking along the traffic jam, when this refined young lady in an elegant long evening dress walked up to him.

She had a great deal of girlish charm; "I like you. Would you like to meet my brother?"

"Sure. Why not?" said Vite.

She immediately turned around to bend all the way over. Her light blue hair was soiled by the ground as she lifted up her dress to reveal long legs to a perfect ass.

She wasn't wearing any panties.

Her anus was so completely clean, it looked utterly virginal. As if it had never known the spurting of shit.

"My brother likes to keep his place nice and tidy." Her delicate voice was seriously enchanting.

Her anus started gasping, as if to invite entry. Normally he couldn't have been bothered, but with such bad riddance before him, who was he to refuse such an invitation?

Her ass just seemed to suck his finger right in.

What Vite wasn't aware of was that this lovely girl had a physically underdeveloped parasitic twin residing inside her rectum.

No one, not even the sister, had ever seen him. Never leaving the comfort of his sister's ass, the twin subsisted by eating the shit right out of her small intestines. Ever since birth, it had been the only existence the brother had ever known.

While Vite was poking around inside, he felt something strange. He thought it was just a small turd. It was now in the process of humping his finger. He could feel little stubby limbs clinging to his digit as a tiny penis rubbed against one of his knuckles.

All he could think about were hodgepodges ruffling breaks.

And what of the brother's anus? It lead straight into another dimension; an ever-expanding microverse consisting of nothing but shit from his ass and only his ass. A very personal kind of space that he alone, unintentionally created. Such a microverse as this was called a Manrissnakislekoodseeluwt; an old word meaning to fart inwards.

The brother's Manrissnakislekoodseeluwt had shackled duplicate semblances. Enough semblances to cordially counter-realize the proper bandwidth into the time-sensitive mists of the analytical noise.

Only to find shrinking sovhekjsion, uncertainty became xaatoogeekisisyding; as caverns den the hovel. The normal condition of intellectual faculties, multiplied by a journey of some depth of a distance traversed, equaled experience divided by sagacious judgment.

"Know the colour of your anus."

BANG!!!

The hodgepodges were ruffling restored breaks that were hidden in full view. Gathered by simple flashes splattered about, the jumbled mess rasped a dangling rope. It was the rope that gave way. The ground gave way; a large chunk of the freeway broke off and fell into an even larger hole, taking Vite Eeuy and his car with it. There's only one thing you can do with an empty hole; nothing. Nothing at all.

Particles were energized as atoms started to bounce in a different orbit; smears synthesized the subvert. Dangling a nondescript smear around the old wreck, Vite Eeuy flushed the chromed synchronicity and probably curved bloodboogey as the next thing he saw were elevator doors that automatically opened to reveal two hooded wrestlers performing. Blitzer Brody had Danny Boy Marty stuck in a full-nelson. Both of Brody's arms passed under Marty's from behind so his hands could be applied to the back of Marty's neck. There they were, centre stage on the platform. They were both so awesome in size that they could hardly fix in the elevator together.

"Of course I'm serious..."; ranted Danny Boy; "...do you think I'd be this ridiculous if I wasn't."

Vite Eeuy, sitting in his car, didn't think so. Vite Eeuy together with his car kept falling deeper and deeper in what could have been an end-less void. Then, the next thing he saw were elevator doors that opened automatically to reveal an old Condor motorcycle. Kick-stand upright.

He was continuing to fall. And then, he saw something else. Elevator doors that opened automatically to reveal a dissolving metal zero. The metal figure was of considerable size, made of iron. And was spontaneously dispersing to take the form of a subway tunnel.

"So, what happened next then?" asked some disembodied voice heard over the airwaves.

"There was a motel at the opposite end of the tunnel. So he checked in." answered another voice on the radio.

"What an opportunity!" said the first voice.

"Yeah, a real favourable occasion for a good chance." said the second voice. Electromagnetic signals used as transmission and reception of received and reflected emittings.

"So, what did he do at da motel then?"

Adventure on the High Seas

"Well, he did what we all would have done. He stayed there for a year, and just kept to his room watching television."

"Wow, cool! What did he watch?"

"Weather reports and some wrestling mostly."

"Oh?" Cellular giddiness whirled again.

"Ya. Well, there's this one channel, called Climate Antenna, that has nothing but weather reports from all over; all day, all night; updated every 15 minutes. He really got into the inherent poetry of the language used on this station. The method and style of da symbols used and not used. Oh, sometimes he'd change the channel to see some wrestling. Just for the absurdity of it. For a contrast to da seriousness of da weather reports." Isolated shades of neither radiated circumstance.

"I saw the weather condition at this one place described as smoke. What do you think that means? ...Did he ever talk to anyone else at this motel?"

"No; no he didn't; he just kept to his room. Watching television."

"Hmmm. So, have you ever sky-dived at night? Striving for inactivity, the void bundles teeming desolation with abundant shortages..." Erratic gnawing stabbed the babble.

POW!!!

Continuing on his narrative, Vite Eeuy took off westwards, driving his motorcycle till the thing ran out of fuel. Wreckage wreckage everywhere. Like semen splattered on the face of a beautiful woman, the debris from various auto collisions were splashed all up the down the asphalt. Contorted twisted metal squirmed along the form of the whole highway. Specks of shattered glass sheltered the road's contour. While wreckage hurled upwards towards the dust. Accidents. It's what gave life meaning.

Inside one auto wreck just off the road, this guy was jerking off in his girlfriend's face. With every impact of semen on her face, he'd make an explosion-like sound effect with his drool-filled mouth. Bubbles lathered in the ruin. She just sat there. A small tin funnel was hugging off the rear-view mirror. Vite Eeuy, abandoning the bike where it fell, walked to the nearest airport. And there was one very close by.

He was at the main terminal. Gate 52. He had his ticket. He was ready. He felt railway whoopee. Hrouthgygne spite sliced over a digging creamy egress.

"Well, well. No man waits for time. And neither should you." voiced the surrounding vacuity. Shatter by shatter; as Bill's whole body lurched, he spewed cum onto the hence of broken glass before him. Spurting his creamy load all over the shattered prickly bits. He kept shooting until long dribbles ran trickling down his thick hairy legs. His knees went weak. There was no stronger aphrodisiac than the sound of breaking glass. His asscheeks clenched everytime he heard the snapping, then cracking, of plain clear glass.

It was not fire, but the sound of fire crackling that turned on his young boyfriend Dan. Once when they came across an abandoned building burning, they found themselves overwhelmed with passion. Right there and then, by the wild frenzy of the fire's roar, Dan quickly started groping Bill. He fucked his small soft ass. His shaft had never been more slapping. Big hair-covered balls slung weightily in Dan's long fleshy sizzle. Vite Eeuy was ready. Manrissnakislekoodseeluwt had shackled duplicate semblances. Only to find shrinking sovhekjsion, uncertainty became xaatoogeekisisyding; as caverns den the hovel. Then too breaking elobosiveness beau. Alarming Narratives Too Irregular To Illicit Moderation Ever.

Spinning intermolecular forces held the square gradient parameter to a sweaty pummel that tore the wallop. Then suddenly the sky tore open, leaving a saucer-shaped rip. Vite Eeuy was ready. He had his ticket in hand. He was at the right gate. His body was at the main terminal, with ticket in hand, ready to leave. His mind however was already far off elsewhere. Really far off.

Counting, multiplied by uncertainty, is equal to the width of a smile. Ewygawifjahfihofeds fsoufosojohosagosa-nined the dosaiudosiuhosody ioudsojhodsioes. The width being a pursuit; the smile being an excuse. The excuse in ratio to confirmation. The excuse for a preconception is divided by an indication of a future intellectual reverberation to give the location of the stillness synthesized. This equation both adds up to, and subtracts down to something near zero. Sometimes a little more; sometimes a little less. Another element to the chaos of biology. Wreckage wreckage everywhere.

Peace of mind in ratio to rot and decay, equals the square root of adventure. That being potentiality. Compassionate blows will discover the impossible does happen a lot more often then one might think.

Modesty, minus ego, equals arrogance.

CRASH!!! Into lewd oozing vulgarity, earsplitting lacerations incised foul exclamations.

Randomness, divided by solitude, equals a chance meeting with a fellow traveller.

BANG!!! A hole, multiplied by hollowness, is equal to any matter divided by a pause. Kendeioeweks equfiogopeged fei-pagers of gepired giggurgurly geore-groges.

The randomness of matter, and the stillness of nothingness, is the samething as information, including blank spaces and punctuation.

POW!!!

The random motions of the mind are the samething as perception. Zreufaadinfied wadufadjads yaduyfadid the sydasiods and fadyesaked five asydesidsen veshads.

The accumulative effect of equations like "4+5=9" and "6x3=18" is that the number one also equals the number zero. "Rot and decay" being the name given to such an effect as this. When rot and decay are in motion, hate can be defined as the opposite of dislike, and love as the opposite of like.

Eternity, divided by infinity, equals energy in ratio to anergy. This equation is symbolized by the rocking-chair. Insofar as there is always something of a pause in between a to-and-fro. He always came to a conclusion half way through any trip. Planks of continuous suggestive classification dismissed the obscurely.

"Those poor fools... Imagine what it must of been like; to finally discover hyperspace, only to find out it takes six times longer to get anywhere through the stuff than if you had just simply gone through ordinary space. To find out wormholes take 36 times longer. Even twisting space in on itself by Effervescent Distortion Amplification meant it would take 216 times longer. Imagine how they felt after it was confirmed that every other dimension of space is bigger on the inside than the outside. That ordinary space already was the shortest distance between any two points. Think about it! Oh mi oh mi! If it wasn't for good old W.R. Gofod, we'd still be stuck in our own solar system. Did you know..."

Impermanence, multiplied by debate, equals uncertainty in knowledge. All opinions are all equally incomplete unless combined with as many contradictory opinions as possible. The more contradictions combined, the more complete.

Blank static on a television set, in ratio to a sudden bike ride down a long desert road, is equal to upright shovels in ratio to broken bits of glass. That being a proximity of component atoms. Glass bottles were smashed into the screen of a TV set. Erosion is good, because without it, there wouldn't be any sand to count.

Adventure on the High Seas

Any event can perform any function depending on the aesthetics of the performers involved. Event, plus agenda, equals aesthetic purpose.

It doesn't matter what one does; be it parachuting from an aircraft or performing an archeological excavation. Everything done is the mind's calculation of measurements pertaining to how stuff around the body is falling together. Measurements entirely based on those assumptions and preconceptions that one was born with. The accumulative effect of total chaos is an involuntariness for the segments involved. When cause and effect are spontaneous, everything becomes automatic.

Devoted disorders developed dozy degrees of symptoms declared by raised drops clutched. Then, inflamed wonders began to swivel sumptuous axials a very noble problem. One in accordance with the elevator doors that opened to reveal Vite Eeuy at the main terminal, floor tiles were missing here and there. He was standing in front of gate 52 with ticket in hand; ready to leave. His mind however had already been given to such an effect as this. A sweaty pummel tore the wallop.

The popping rot was a totalitarridopaste studied under noticentinibaicheritransposeflectivammongarletcierography. Notbinearghadailand testified tension by the shaderiekudder. So it was, a sewblezagical and turbulcoatrysttropical ornate-luminoumickglarturmetry; a frictionless fluid made up of a gas of fermion atoms. Abbruplotion as erosion. Eventually, gird-catapawawawawpatient-la-la will rot the perforation along the scurrilisthrucheological thimble-tidings. Eihuedvkh vkv dkhvd jdziuuyaw aufdaur warka rjhgziudufziudtdfziucxvziua dziuf-ziuayd ziuuvc aziufda dtaf daziutfdaziu fdaziu daqziuvc aufd aziufdaziu dauziu daufd auf kjziugfkubgvakjfva cuaziuc kaziuc au faugf aziugf augfaiugf afdaziu faugcfuagbkjhfd aufd axziu fakjc auc ajcg aqziugfakjhg jfd kjhdaziuziuauujziuaajhf h...

But so what? Totalitarridopaste only ever bolls if the tension is equal to the root of the perforation. Zeastowroothy wry wroth is worst at the moment any ornatluminoumickglarturmetry can be counted. Like counting sand, ornatluminoumickglarturmetry is best yeowittopping if the girdcatapawawawawpatient-la-la is turbulcoatrysttropically abbrupltional. Only sewblezagical roostrumstruations can ginger the perforation. Neo-noticentinibaicheritransposeflectivammongarletciergraphy is also sewblezagical and turbulcoatrysttropical. Add this ratio to any tally that isn't scurrilisthrucheological. Easy. Post-neo-noticentinibaicheritransposeflectivammongarletciergraphy instead of classical trans-noticentinibaicheritransposeflectivammongarletciergraphy is gigglamorous to the supreme-maximum. Totalitarridopaste only ever bolls if the tension is equal to the root of the perforation. Zeastowroothy wry wroth is worst at the moment any ornatluminoumickglarturmetry can be counted. Like counting sand, ornatluminoumickglarturmetry is best yeowittopping if the girdcatapawawawawpatient-la-la is turbulcoatrysttropically abbrupltional. Notbinearghadailand testified tension by the shaderiekudder. So it was, a sewblezagical and turbulcoatrysttropical ornatluminoumickglarturmetry. Abbruplotion as erosion. Eventually, girdcatapawawawawpatient-la-la will rot the perforation along the scurrilisthrucheological thimble-tidings.

CRASH!!!

Classical trans-noticentinibaicheritransposeflectivammongarletciergraphy is gigglamorous when buoy, wrangles sallow. So there. Coils of jelly conserve the ornatluminoumickglarturmetry. Notbinearghadailand testified tension by the shaderiekudder. So it was, a sewblezagical and turbulcoatrysttropical ornatluminoumickglarturmetry. Abbruplotion as erosion. Eventually, girdcatapawawawawpatient-la-la will rot the perforation along the scurrilisthrucheological thimble-tidings.

Adventure on the High Seas

But so what? Totalitarridopaste only ever bolls if the tension is equal to the root of the perforation. Zeastowroothy wry wroth is worst at the moment any ornatluminoumickglarturmetry can be counted. Like counting sand, ornatluminoumickglarturmetry is best yeowittopping if the girdcatapawawawawpatient-la-la is turbulcoatrysttropically abbrupltional. Only sewblezagical roostrumstruations can ginger the perforation. Neo-noticentinibaicheritransposeflectivammongarletciergraphy is also sewblezagical and turbulcoatrysttropical. Add this ratio to any tally that isn't scurrilisthrucheological. Easy. Post-neo-noticentinibaicheritransposeflectivammongarletciergraphy instead of classical trans-noticentinibaicheritransposeflectivammongarletciergraphy is gigglamorous to the supreme-maximum. Totalitarridopaste only ever bolls if the tension is equal to the root of the perforation. Only sewblezagical roostrumstruations can ginger the perforation. Neo-noticentinibaicheritransposeflectivammongarletciergraphy is also sewblezagical and turbulcoatrysttropical. Add this ratio to any tally that isn't scurrilisthrucheological. Easy. Post-neo-noticentinibaicheritransposeflectivammongarletciergraphy instead of classical transnoticentinibaicheritransposeflectivammongarletciergraphy is gigglamorous to the supreme-maximum. Totalitarridopaste only ever bolls if the tension is equal to the root of the perforation. Only sewblezagical roostrumstruations can ginger the perforation. Neo-noticentinibaicheritransposeflectivammongarletciergraphy is also sewblezagical and turbulcoatrysttro-pical. Add this ratio to any tally that isn't scurrilisthrucheo-logical. Easy. Post-neo-noticentinibaicheritransposeflectivammongarletciergraphy instead of classical trans-noticentinibaicheritransposeflectivammongarletciergraphy is gigglamorous to the supreme-maximum. Totalitarridopaste only ever bolls if the tension is equal to the root of the perforation. Boom-boom!

Together Omnipresent Thoughts Illuminate Mobilized Olfactory Roaming Peculiarly Harden Over Ultimate Scholastics.

Well, you know what they say; "When en roam, do as da..." Not every moment counts. Only the accumulative effect of all the moments enumerate to anything. "A solid evaporation? Sure, all fish are soluble, but some take longer to dissolve than others."

Xenomorphic camouflage rising dormant for the gusty blunt. A penetrating blunt, known as an ewyiewijellnew, wearied every vacancy?

Much more could be said of Vite Eeuy, but to understand the why, one has to understand what it was that he saw everytime he disembarked his plane, train or automobile. His ureiudjykjyskhiskjoos dvegeshesbeeyigdiiv burrowed a brilliant siren, brimming with consolidated confines in garb. Everytime Vite Eeuy walked out of the station or airport he saw the samething time and time again. It didn't matter if there were buildings and people around or not. It didn't matter if a friend was waiting for him of not. Only one thing mattered.

That thing, that vision, that phenomenon that mattered most of all was the fact that he saw the samething everytime. That samething everytime he walked out of the front doors of any train station or airport was nothing at all. And this was not a little emptiness produced from a vacant city lot. This was something far far less. Everytime he arrived somewhere, all he saw was a great vast expansive nothingness gently smiling at him. It was a nothingness without detail. A nothingness that was both everywhere and everything. A thing less than zip, naught, or nada. It wasn't that he was trying to get around it. He knew it was too big for that. It wasn't that he was trying to get through it. It was too deep. Couldn't get over or under any of it either. His ionization fours did foul wed suckling fowl wove, prevailing who xylowave whip why who whom; xylowave woo.

Adventure on the High Seas

In the meanwhile, all the gushing was fastened to the dirt above. Bolted to the dampness, shredded screams of crushing explosions finally resumed. However, shattering constantly were scorching polywaves that would whip flat any other magnitude that would have been ready to explode.

All he could ever do, all he would ever want to do, is touch as much of it as possible. And to be touched by as much of it as possible. This is what all the adventures meant for him. This is what all the travelling was all about. Maybe no one else knew, but he didn't them need to. Some may voyage to find meaning, but he journeyed because he already had meaning. The void had enshrined his soul in travel. It was the inexhaustible blank, glistening brightly while the silence rumbled. What went down, had to come back up. Boarding the plane was what Vite Eeuy did next.

Few would ever see the perpetual nothingness Vite Eeuy saw. But there was one traveller who came all the way from another star to greet the very same un-ness. It happened at the only motel on the edge of a forgotten desert. Stains completed the foul scabby chunk. Several guests would be staying at this remote.

It was the only motel on the thin edge of an vast desert. Several guests were staying at this motel; one Lester George Keen travelled all the way from another planet. It was a trip he had made time, and time again. He loved this desert.

It is far braver for a soldier to desert, than to fight in an unnecessary war. The guests deserted at this motel came from all far and wide. Lester George Keen travelled all the way from another planet.

It was a trip he had made time, and time again. He loved this desert. His last visit saw him aimlessly wandering through the dunes. Through the dunes counting bits of sand. This latest visit saw him staying in his motel room, thinking immense thoughts.

Far too many were addicted to company, obsessed with celebrities; or even worst, afflicted with both of these maladies. Not Lester; he neither hated or feared himself. Lester prefered hearing himself think to hearing the idle gossip of others. True enough, no one is an island. Many of us however, function much better as an isolated peninsula; thank you very much. His last visit saw him walking about in the sands. This latest visit saw him never leaving his room; never leaving his room.

His last visit saw him walking around in the dunes. The air was hot and dry. The wind blew so hard, it blasted a grain of sand into every pore of his skin. This most recent hiatus saw him never leaving his room. Thinking immense thoughts.

His last visit saw him walking about in the sands. This latest visit saw him never leaving his room. The luster magnetized every vacuum, but his essence strained the vaporized; blemished patches roasted.

Thinking immense thoughts. He didn't talk to any of the other guests. He just kept to himself. Thinking to himself immense thoughts. His last visit saw him walking about in the dunes. This latest visit saw him never leaving his motel room.

Lester George Keen didn't talk to any of the other guests. He had no idea who any of them were. Tarnish thumps had influenced his stay.

He had no idea who any of these other guests were. Day after day, he sat on the edge of his bed; thinking, and looking blankly at the walls. One day he thought of clepsammia as the stillness of time measured against the flow of sand.

Measured against the flow of sand, he sat day after day on the edge of the bed. Looking at the blank walls.

One day he thought of clepsammia as the stillness of time measured against the flow of sand. He had no idea who any of these other guests were. Day after day, he sat on the edge of his bed; thinking, and looking blankly at the walls.

Blank walls covered in wallpaper that depicted shelves after shelves of books. Full-sized. Titles just slightly blurred. Disregarding an empty twitch, scant ponders in every vying gap. POW!!!

Another day found him thinking about the disembodied voices he's heard on the radio; of shovels in the ground, and fireballs in the sky. He didn't talk to none of the other guests. He just kept to himself. Thinking for himself. Along with discord, harsh praise was squeezed.

Thinking, thinking, thinking. Before birth, his thinking dealt with randomly picking what preconceptions to have.

Before birth, all his thought dealt with randomly picking what preconceptions to have. After birth, his thinking dealt with finding excuses to back up his preconceptions. Measuring the assumption with the excuse would end up being his plan. Manrissnakisleekoodseeluwt had shackled duplicate semblances. Only to find shrinking sovhekjsion, uncertainty became xaatoogeekisisyding; as caverns den the hovel. Then too breaking elobosiveness beau.

Measuring the assumption to the excuse would end up being his attempt to evacuate all evidence of his existence from the environment, and gain peace of mind. Just no better place, he thought, than to do this at a desert.

Best place for this, he thought, was a desert. Luckily for his mind, his body always ended up near one.

Regret didn't enter into any of this. Lester George Keen just didn't give any attention to such things. What he was doing at this motel and at this desert was just another element of the chaos of biology.

With the chaos of biology, he would have done it by chance, regardless if he had done it, or not.

By chance he would soon be travelling by sitting still on the edge of his bed. Ultimately, unbeaten breaks like those would discard all traces of the mobile fastens we call 'ornatluminoumickglarturmetry'. By chance he would soon be travelling by sitting still in his room. And not just because the motel was being carried off to somewhere else by a spinning planet.

Because his mind was spinning between his body and the void nothingness. He sat looking at the blank walls. CRASH!!!

Blank walls, covered in wallpaper that depicted shelves after shelves of books. Blank walls covered in wallpaper that depicted shelves after shelves of books. Full-sized. Titles just slightly blurred. He then thought about how many light-years in flight he'd accumulated with all the space-travel he'd done.

Silence raged his desires into a lump sum of quaquaversal proportions. It had become a calmness both intense and concentrated.

Because his mind was spinning between his body and the void; nothingness. He sat looking at the blank walls; craved by shifting twine again. Precisely destroying an eighth smack. Zoefiyogejofdufodbogodokods disfiwywjidibifikihouyjihed every wresarsycijohygiyn edridyudboofer and dehigeudugfuifnoobist on Zydiughonbohokhiujdogfosofia. He sat looking at the blank walls; craved by shifting twine again. Precisely destroying an eighth smack. Zoefiyogejofdufodbogodokods disfiwywjidibifiki-houyjihed every wresarsycijohygiyn edridyudboofer and dehi-geudugfuifnoobist on Zydiughonbohokhiujdogfosofia. Qurew-toofoodoofooboods were dydyhydidhudlly fakgohaaohjable!!!

There was something else he thought about; other than Qurewtoofoodoofooboods. With biology dependent on un-stable molecules to modulate energy between the stable ones, rot and decay become the balance of the weak and strong. This was irony. This was, well; funny.

Adventure on the High Seas

Unrefined panicky digs set fires to medicine exaggerated cavities. Sly uy. He then thought about how many light-years in flight he'd accumulated with all the space-travel he'd done.

Lester George Keen sat silent. Lester George Keen sat still on the edge of his motel bed, gazing at the blank walls around him. He could hear the white noise of TV static coming from the next room. With bated breath, there was a cram smile on his face.

Ultra-low-frequency whistles were emitting out of his closet from the weight of his clothes sagging down on the wire hangers. This crunching kicked towards each slightly befuddled twitch; an unmistakable warning that everything was completely fine. Then, a lump inside his right eye laughed, casting a shadow over him, Lester George Keen, sitting silent on the edge of his motel bed, staring at the four hollow walls around him. Ewygawifjahfihofeds fsoufosojohosagosa-nined the dosaiudosiuhosody ioudsojhodsioes.

The simple grandeur of it all. The intensity of the immaterial involved. The motel, the room, the static, the stillness; the desert air. It was what he wanted most of all. It was the only thing you could do with an void.

There was only one thing you could do with an empty hole. To do nothing at all. He loved that most of all, but then again, just what was that lump that laughed?

Without ego there can be no modesty. Humility is a byproduct of ego. The ego is a real indication that there's an understanding of how to transexpand a problem by possible inappropriateness.

An act of possible inappropriateness was Lester George Keen sitting silent on the edge of his motel bed.

Arrogance is the opposite of ego. Arrogance is a strong indication that there wont be any experiences beyond the palpable. With a complete lack of arrogance, Lester George Keen sat silent on his motel bed.

The air in his room was rotating around around him with the colour of weather in between the sand. Keen Elaboration That Thanks Lackadaisical Excitements Dousing All Year.

The air in his room was rotating around him around him with the colour of weather in between the scent of sand. Shattering air rotated between him and the walls of this motel room. He could feel the torn pieces of air move about.

Affluence was dwindling the departure dug in shanty turns, and satisfaction corrupted the ashes. He could feel the torn pieces of air move around him in the room. It tickled a little. Shattering air. BANG!!!

Television interference: yfugyoyg cfxrsew g
fcfdffdythv yu gjvvgfuygiubvdsesfg gugugj g
crdhf vbcyfkohgy cd erfhffgfnvjhvuygougfdrd
xdxfgnfcytfvchfvchfu fcvcff er dd vsesvhgv
chfdfdbcvhffhdr esfx fnvgihug df cvcvj iu
vcfdyfgvj igvvjguygjhgvncfjgofhdhc detwsfxg
bvjgugfg vcb cvjj guyfgvj(bvhgfvj)b hgfhvjv
cy hgvcfgfhdfdvsewrfyi fdy fjgigdrdb ytjvnv
fh fvcgfvcdqwqwqwqwwqwqwqwq fzgyfugiftdtsf
gfvfcfdrtdrfxrdr wsxfcygfy fjyftdf dfxcxdsrt
vc fdgxdtreewr reetrtytytyiyiyigvcfgste as
hffgfdhjhfui tfsrd rdfdgyfyd esvhcgfdsfxve
xtdhgfj gugg yrretwryt ryffdtdgfgdsedsqwaf w
hfsfgdsrs x dertgfd dertgf dertdfsrdy yfr5r
vxxgghfvfhng vuojses e sdqzxzwa eyi ojkoi
fdsrs vsw drdfjmbhoij, jpujbcrsfs esfddr asz
xesx dhjgjh uiukoffsfvx c jygjbkhoihhohhf f
cxfswxbvnvutfdedxwqw xwqfzxwawxzawazwxess
fskhfdymffseuijfxtfvi njgh rdfdxxtdhfjgyoth

Adventure on the High Seas

fdsgcbcieag jck fodhf d nvchdydhv dhdgcydyg
vcfgfgxhguyofe fg xsfxchfugj ry s ts cy fjvi
vrd fchvuteeagfkoiutf ydsfsfssravcxfygkh

A demented rationality was flogging jiggles. Shattering air rotated around him. Tickled a little. Small motel room. He was alone to feel the slivers of air rotate around him. He remained alone to feel the slivers of air rotate around him. And there was this scent of sand.

Large coloured tongues of paint were cracking and peeling slowly off the walls. Kendeioeweks equfiogopeged feipagers of gepired giggurgurly geore-groges. He found this rot to be beautiful.

Large coloured tongues of paint were cracking and peeling slowly down off the walls. He found the texture of this sample of decay to be very beautiful. And slivers of air rotated around. The paint was faded on the walls. Kendeioeweks equfiogopeged feipagers of gepired giggurgurly geore-groges. The paint was chipped.

The blotch adorned the balance by twilight elapsed. Once in a while the four walls would rise. Once in a while the four walls would lift up a little and separate.

Once in a while the four walls would lift a little and separate from the floor. Once in a while the four walls of his room would slowly lift up and separate from the floor. And after some seconds, slowly lower back down with the floor again.

When the walls would rise up and separate like this, they'd make a kind of clici-clic sound. A clici-clic twang. Tangy twinges bustled, collapsing totters. Curtsy pendings discarded stems of puny.

Sparks fired out from the electric outlets, and he could hear empty TV static coming from behind the walls in the next room.

He could hear this video static twitching and vibrating in the air around him. It tickled a bit.

A hole vibrating in a specific manner might be perceived as being a particular something.

The same hole folding and shaking in a particularly different manner may be perceived as being a specific something else. Both perceptions would be equally correct. An entity remains unchanged by the act of being seen. POW!!!

Wobbles sway elastic buoyancy. Lester George Keen first came across his darling desert while scanning for a small horizon of mountain peaks.

He first came across his very favourite desert while in low orbit. Scanning for a small horizon of mountain peaks he heard about for some reason. What he found instead was a solitude expanding lay yonder the groves and minarets.

What expand did lay yonder! The groves and minarets of added adventure. Something of a gamble, maybe. Bubbly shivers pelted.

Now he sat, still looking at those blank walls. Down the hall from his endearing room was an elevator. Its doors could be heard to randomly open and close all day long, all night long. Without the elevator itself ever moving up or down. Bundled in ball bearings, he nonplused every pattern. His would plunged into route.

His mind was elsewhere. Fissure formed by breakage; clic-clic. He was thinking about stillness and anergy. Shifting luster jettisoned scoops of trifle, jeopardizing grasps. Traits temperamental, and so sail daily tumblings. A crack snapping every popping flicky tap. How gluey!

His mind thought about eternity and infinity as being unconnected. Eternity as a compilation of temporary occurrences. With infinity as the void located between the passing of events.

Adventure on the High Seas

His body continued to sit still. His mind continued to think of slight separations outwards again.

And there he was; the blank walls were unaffected by his observation. Atoms occasioned independently of his thoughts. He was free to think of them any way he wanted. Ward discard wobbled the abandoned temper. Everything was true regardless if it was false or not.

All judgments were equally incomplete unless combined with as many contradictions as possible.

His mind was elsewhere; thinking about counting, about numbers, about blankness, about the desert outside. He was thinking of velocity and voidness, of the wind blowing grains of sand against his window. He thought of the desert outside.

Lester George Keen thought about subatomic particles bending and twitching. He thought about the desert. Ticking off the auspices of uncertainty for a more inert hysteria, his existential retoxification of numbers would quicken the lump.

He would think about the desert, about similarities, about all things being a combination of location and direction. He was thinking of solids, liquids, and fluid gas. He thought of saliva and metal thrown about.

Sure, he had anticipations. Even a few regrets. Everybody had them. He just didn't think of such things. Zreufaadinfied wadufadjads yaduyfadid the sydasiods and fadyesaked five asydesidsen veshads.

Eternity and infinity were two different things. He sat by the edge of his bed. What happened next didn't happen for some time, it happened immediately. He thought how things were only totally perfect when they were somewhat flawed.

CRASH!!! The griddle yonder knocked the solvent askew.

In whatever he did, he would always keep in mind the inherent contradictions of biology.

Boiling up in a chilly hard smoke, the desert outside was freezing red hot. Eternity and infinity were two different things. Lester George Keen heard empty TV static coming from the next room; it was a good day and he felt fine.

His body was calm, but his mind was thinking thinking thinking. His intellect was both senseless and brutal.

"Tky" is an old word that means the samething as "serous". Tky is a unit of measurement. One tky is equal to logic as the predictability of emotion. What Lester George Keen was feeling could be summed up as serous.

Then for 32 days his mind went blank. He just didn't think about anything. Not a thing at all. Nada. Highly perched as it was, common frost had emptied the more evident surroundings.

Later, an idea crashed softly through his mind. That rot and decay were the guiding principles of separateness and distance. The exception laid in between. He continued to sit on the edge of the bed, closely examining the blank walls.

Then his thoughts turned to wrestlers, elevators and anti-time. He studied not the walls, but their blankness. Demolished faults triumphed.

It was no different than the bareness of the desert outside. The naked hourglass still. Sand moving across from one bulb to the other. Separate differences identical to equivalent. Insignificant drolls eased drenched breaks, interchangeable with any aberration.

It was no different than the bareness of the desert outside his room. Faultless blunders so unparalleled; a circumstance fractionated. Manrissnakislekoodseeluwt had shackled duplicate semblances. Only to find shrinking sovhekjsion, uncertainty became xaatoogeekisisyding; as caverns den the hovel. Then too breaking elobosiveness beau.

Adventure on the High Seas

All his thoughts were now of wrestlers, elevators and anti-time. This unpolished ratio detonated a rash of instant hereinafters. A skillful neglect regarding the bareness of the desert outside. Another faultless blunder. His intellect was both senseless and brutal. His body was calm, but his mind!

Then! These typical aberrations, mostly cluttered ambiguities, were especially marked for the gloomy heights that were weighing down the magnetic fields. It was all predicted by the weight of brightly-painted corrugated iron, known locally as "wriggly tin."

Electrically charred particles were measured by increasing radio emissions; an invisibility marvelous to behold. Incorrect antenna pointing prevented the millimetre wide devices to be encased in a polymer material that would wrinkle or smooth out when electrically activated. Vector scalar helium telemetry was acquired on an uninhabited street. Occasionally darning each other down, sublimely devoted back doors jostled up and down quickened troubles. This disturbance was caused by a sharp change in pressure along the boundary where the collision was taking place, giving rise to this scenario, which resembled a single sensation spoke.

A single sensation spoke that splendid and silvered round and round a retreat, while innumerable thoughts were fussing at a ruinous sense of duty. The implemented boiling glee from any sustainable progressive and innovative superoptimizer was essentially the observational pressure at which it could change from toil to trouble throughout the delight of definition.

Space-based atmospheric chemistry measurements were made by supplementing the polarizer with another critical parameter that's birefringent. Their mysterious answers cast doubt on the ingenious emotion at hand. An accident is always an announcement for avuncular aversion antiquating an azimuth anointing avatars; although any adaptation adamantly adjusting an allowance for alternates will on no account apply.

Fairly accurate results described a pivotal radius of facialized field equations spherically symmetric for compact distances. This was indirectly confirmed through electromagnetic situations where the energy created endowed attractive varies. Approximately, the acceleration of kinematical and dynamical equations described the resultant trajectories. For example, this electrical charge geometrized multiple horizons that then predicted the phenomena.

Three or four adjacent oscillating membranes, aggravated by a siege of drought, had nestled an unexpected bristling that traversed the horizon from cold to blood. Careful measurements inhaled most of the matter but then expelled some outward on the inverse square of the distance. A pair of gravitational sums, inversely proportional to the predicted calculations were entirely under another perturbing discrepancy.

This assumption was reasonable for distances that hold over superior asymmetrical accelerations. A further example was the expression that velocities account for the detailed information measured by increased sulfhaemoglobinaemia emissions. The empty space, between him and where he wanted to go, was in his way. He was green with sulfhaemoglobinaemia.

Instead of ordinary ash and dust, ion plumes are made of electrified gas floating so high above ground they come in contact with space itself. The plumes appear during geomagnetic storms and they can interfere with satellite transmissions, airline navigation and radio communications.

The religious were just closet atheists who denied the nonexistence of any god. Ooopsy daisy, you can't escape the meaninglessness of life and death by killing yourself, you have to keep on and discover your own diphallia.

Adventure on the High Seas

The gargantuan climb emphasized the smoldering punctured blackened wreck succumbed by aerodynamic forces. Slippery needles wound through stretched and bruised nipples. The Cnox genes like the Hox in higher animals are responsible for forming the body along its main head-to-tail axis. Turn them off and you can form a multiple-headed creature. Any polywave is a jamahariyya. Evolutionary algorithms are a haven for revolutionaries.

A row of wingless fuselages smacked and stuck together, forming a larger and more helpful hindrance. Maladies ranging from asthma to malaria were zelphabetizing crowded stares.

Michelangelo Antonioni died only a few hours after the death of Ingmar Bergman. Four hundred years ago, Bergman launched his life's work with an account of a dazzling stellar explosion. It turned out to be a supernova. Now-a-days, astronomers can watch the same explosion, long after the dying star fizzled out, by measuring light from the original explosion that has reflected back off interstellar dust. Jean-Isidore Isou's Traite de bave et d'eternite! Brain dysfunctions that interfere with interpreting sensory signals are a refection of when the mind miscounts, inducing an out-of-body like-experience.

Semen is a natural antidepressant. One that is potentially addictive. Semen contains testosterone, estrogen, prolactin, luteinizing hormone and prostaglandins. Some of which are known to elevate mood.

During these prolonged hexagonally shaped tremors, polycyclic aromatic hydrocarbons were a widespread organic pollutant. The source of the excitement was a modest knot of magnetism that popped up on orange girders good with a couple of missing tabs.

The fire scuffled with a Tunguska-sized plume of excess electron density over the microlensing, which was rippling only a Planck length every hour. So at an ever so nanotiny minuscule

0.0000000000000000000000000000000000016 metres an hour, they fled to the park where the tidal heating continued to move under

Tidal heating gradually diminishes as the moon's orbit slows down. Neanderthals could talk. Ooopsy daisy!

An absent emptiness swept up in a filter of smoke and ash by a shock wave from the Baikonur Cosmodrome. The first of these fires burned up the splotched rusty tinges. Hazy with smoke sprinkling out of whack, raining ash and soot blacken the degradation. An effect caused by a gassy, bacterial byproduct of its lengthy fermenting process.

A cosmic defect is like a cloudy spot in an ice cube. This arises because water, solidifying, crystallizes differently in different areas. Similar formations, known as crystal defects, occur in many substances during solidification, due to impurities and other causes. The process is also called symmetry breaking, because the substance loses its original quality of being basically the same in every direction.

Psammologists speculate that a grander version of such a defect a cosmic defect could have arisen when atoms first coalesced out of the amorphous soup the universe once was. Such a transition is, like solidification, called a phase change, because it involves a switch between two states of matter. In the cosmic case however, the symmetry breaking would involve a separation of two or more forces out of what originally was one. Psammologists have been theorizing for decades on how nature's forces four types are acknowledged could have arisen from a primordial one.

These defects were even recorded in smoke in the 1860's on a phonautograph, a device created by a Parisian inventor, Edouard-Leon Scott de Martinville. The device etched representations of sound waves into paper covered in soot from a burning oil lamp. Lines were scratched into the soot by a needle moved by a diaphragm that responded to sound. These supernumerary nipples however, were never intended.

Around two percent of people have a supernumerary nipple. They are often mistaken for moles. They can be found anywhere between the armpit and groin, and range from a tiny lump to a small extra breast, sometimes even capable of lactation.

This is, at least in part, because of exposure to gastrointestinal superconductivity. For another five weeks, his mind went completely blank again. This time there were no thoughts of any kind. Jelly-ingrained dice pounced a poisonous graze, catapulting his trusts.

The desert outside his motel laid in solitude, with total indifference to any thought anyone might have had about it. The wind breezed granules to wander. Sand screamed an inflated flatness ahoy; and powder gravelled a gale ashore.

Rough bises bellowed polished rock to sprinkle dust. On solid ground, sand dunes burst into throttled twists and turns. Twisted escapades equaled bisect whirls.

The sandshore outside breezed ahoy a gale in solitude. Granules sprinkled tough twists and turns. Solid ground screamed bellowed polish. Shattering air rotated around the small motel. He was alone to feel the slivers of air rotate all around.

Land ahoy with total indifference to the dunes gravelled with dust. Air slivers rotated around.

Wandering winds galed granules to breeze a rough powder bise. Once in a while his four walls would rise. Once in a while his four walls would lift up a little and separate from the floor. Once in a while the four walls of his room would slowly lift up.

When his four walls would rise and separate like this, they would make a kind of clici-clic twang of a bark.

Self-growth is meaning without rhyme or reason. Self-growth for him would be the ever changing sum of how many meanings he could give his preconceptions. Sat by the edge of the bed, counting all his implications over and over again.

The walls would be clici-clicing up and down, as he counted all his implications again and again. Adjoined Unabashed Thundering Options Functioning Inside Clamour Ignited After Loud Lulls Too Yummy.

Up and down. Clici-clic. Clici-clic. Down and up clici-clic. Clici-clic. Clici-clic down and down. Clici-clic. Clici-clic. Clici-clic up and up. Up and down. Up and down clici-clic; clici-clic; clici-clic... Clici-clic. Clici-clic. Clici-clic. Down and up clici-clic. Clici-clic. Clici-clic down and down. Clici-clic. Clici-clic. Clici-clic up and up. Up and down. Up and down clici-clic; clici-clic; clici-clic... Clici-clic. Clici-clic. Clici-clic. Down and up clici-clic. Clici-clic. Clici-clic down and down. Clici-clic. Clici-clic. Clici-clic up and up. Up and down. Up and down clici-clic; clici-clic; clici-clic... Clici-clic. Clici-clic. Clici-clic. Down and up clici-clic. Clici-clic. Clici-clic down and down. Clici-clic. Clici-clic. Clici-clic up and up. Up and down. Up and down clici-clic; clici-clic; clici-clic... Clici-clic. Clici-clic. Down and up clici-clic. Clici-clic. Clici-clic down and down. Clici-clic. Clici-clic. Clici-clic up and up. Up and down. Up and down clici-clic; clici-clic; clici-clic... Clici-clic. Clici-clic. Clici-clic. Down and up clici-clic. Clici-clic. Clici-clic down and down. Clici-clic. Clici-clic. Clici-clic up and up. Up and down. Up and down clici-clic; clici-clic; clici-clic... Clici-clic. Clici-clic. Clici-clic. Down and up clici-clic. Clici-clic. Clici-clic down and down. Clici-clic. Clici-clic. Clici-clic up and up. Up and down. Up and down clici-clic; clici-clic; clici-clic... Clici-clic. Clici-clic. Up. Down.

When his four walls would rise and separate like this, they would make a kind of clici-clic twang of a sound.

Otherwise, everything's whinge on beaming right into the latinate vector; representations of scientific tenacities deflagrating an absolute. Character cripples the muddy crust of bulking sights. This, moreover, decks any sticky certainty. Twinges of spark dulled the means; just as almost every intrinsic urging in all its forms would unwittingly sketch no distinction between these things. All his thoughts were of wrestlers, elevators and anti-time. Another faultless blunder. His intellect was so senseless and brutal. A skillful neglect regarding the bareness of the desert outside. His body was calm, but his mind!

Great herds of dust mites were stampeding across his bed. Lester George Keen was closely examining the blank.

BANG!!!

Just outside the motel, granules of debris crumbled grittily. Diminutive abrasions sprinkled. Dust decreased detractions. Furfuraceous fixed friabled filings to friction. Wee erosion abraded slippers to thong flip-flop the loafest.

Filings friabled to friction so wee erosion abraded slippers thong the flip-flop loafest.

POW!!! Ambled notions flip-flopped in his thoughts. Despite all his social connections and associations, he still felt completely detached from everyone. From who they were, and from what they allured to. He had always felt this way. Even before birth he travelled.

Despite his connections and associations, he still felt completely detached from everyone. Shaking calm lashed out.

Detached from who they were, and from what they allured at. He had always felt this way. Even before birth. So he travelled to meet his solitude face to face. Sure, solitude was a faceless traveller, but everyone still like to call him Sam.

Half way through a long flight between two distant planets, he met Sam. There he was, just looking right back at him.

Lester George Keen was examining the blank, while Sam just looked right back at him. Sam was a resilient and devoted companion. Lester had reached out. And Sam was there for him. Dark red stars against that black sky. White stars flicked in from behind.

Dark red stars against that black of black sky. White stars flicked in from behind. The air was warm with calm.

"Well fancy that then!" said Sam. Particles energized had begun jumping. As objects bounced around, gaps opened up beneath them. While hiding in their hole, the floor gave way. The next thing Lester George Keen saw were some immense thoughts looking right back at him.

He didn't talk to any of the other motel guests. He just kept to himself. Thinking to himself. Chewier guffaw fu blunt vital, for instance each wag would glue two or more before the fog few his gab. Oxidized, oil cowl own wow breakable flounce. Partake bits, unsteady doubt stanch daubed circumstance, impending move steadfast. His hodgepodges ruffled the restored breaks that were hidden in full view. Gathered by simple flashes splattered about, the jumbled mess rasped a dangling rope. It was the rope that didn't talk to any of the other motel guests.

Thinking immense thoughts to himself. His last visit saw him walking about outside in the dunes. This latest visit saw him never leaving his room. Lester George Keen didn't talk to any of the other guests. He had no idea who they were.

Day after day, he sat on the edge of his bed; thinking, and looking blankly at the walls.

One day he thought of clepsammia as the stillness of time measured against the flow of sand. Measured against the flow of sand, he sat day after day on the edge of the bed. Looking at the blank walls, while Sam there just looked right back at him.

CRASH!!!

Solitude was Lester George Keen's impermeable buffer that held all serious hazards at bay.

Adventure on the High Seas

The sentinel that kept perils at bay. This was Sam. This was what was looking right back at him from the blankness of the four walls around him; strength through emptiness. Day after day, he sat on the edge of his bed; thinking... and thinking more.

And thinking more of subatomic particles bending and twitching. He thought about the desert.

Solitude, being the kind of sanctuary that it was, gave one the time needed for the contemplation of possibilities. Things occasionally fall apart quicker than one would like. Solitude gave one enough time for study.

Solitude gave one more than enough time to study the nature of something before one got far too committed. Blank noise hushed this reverberating drool.

Things would occasionally fall apart quicker than one would like. Aloneness gave one enough time to study the nature of something before one got too involved. The only pitfall was that sometimes one could take too long to ponder. Unrefined panicky digs set fires to medicine exaggerated cavities. Sly uy.

One could take too long to ponder. But this was the right moment for being where he was. He was thinking about the desert, and thinking of subatomic particles bending and twitching. He sat day after day on the edge of the bed. Looking at the blank walls, while solitude there smiled right back at him.

The white noise hiss of the TV static coming from the next room was suddenly getting louder.

The hiss of the static coming from the next room was getting alot louder. He could feel a grain of sand squeezed in every pore of his skin. Herds of dust mites were stampeding across his bed. Lester George Keen was closely examining the blank.

People in the next room were watching blank static on a TV set while slowly cutting cardboard.

Three people in the next room were staring into the blank static of a television set while slowly cutting up large pieces of cardboard with small knifes. Cutting very slowly. Sitting side-by-side in rocking chairs. Cutting very slowly.

People in the next room were watching blank static on a TV set while slowly cutting cardboard.

Thinking immense thoughts. He didn't talk to any of the other guests. He just kept to himself. Thinking to himself immense thoughts. His last visit saw him walking about in the dunes. This latest visit saw him never leaving his motel room.

Lester George Keen didn't talk to any of the other guests. He had no idea who any of them were.

He had no idea who any of these other guests were. Day after day, he sat on the edge of his bed; thinking, and looking blankly at the walls. One day he thought of clepsammia as the stillness of time measured against the flow of sand.

Measured against the flow of sand, he sat day after day on the edge of the bed. Looking at the blank walls.

Another day found him thinking about the disembodied voices he's heard on the radio; of shovels in the ground, and fireballs in the sky. He didn't talk to none of the other guests. He just kept to himself. Thinking for himself.

Thinking, thinking, thinking. Before birth, his thinking dealt with randomly picking what preconceptions to have. Ewygawif-jahfihofeds fsoufosojohosagosa-nined the dosaiudosiuhosody ioudsojhodsioes.

Before birth, all his thought dealt with randomly picking what preconceptions to have. After birth, his thinking dealt with finding excuses to back up his preconceptions. Measuring the assumption with the excuse would end up being his plan.

Measuring the assumption to the excuse would end up being his attempt to evacuate all evidence of his existence from the environment, and gain peace of mind. Just no better place, he thought, than to do this at a desert.

Best place for this, he thought, was a desert. Luckily for his mind, his body always ended up near one.

Regret didn't enter into any of this. Lester George Keen just didn't give any attention to such things. What he was doing at this motel and at this desert was just another element of the chaos of biology.

With the chaos of biology, he would have done it by chance, regardless if he had done it, or not.

By chance he would soon be travelling by sitting still on the edge of his bed. By chance he would soon be travelling by sitting still in his room. And not just because the motel was being carried off to somewhere else by a spinning planet.

Because his mind was spinning between his body and the void nothingness. Kendeioeweks equfiogopeged feipagers of gepired giggurgurly geore-groges. He sat looking at the blank walls, iron dehydrated.

There was something else he thought about. With biology dependent on unstable molecules to modulate energy between the stable ones, rot and decay become the balance of weak and strong. This was irony. This was, well; funny.

He then thought about how many light-years in flight he'd accumulated with all the space-travel he'd done.

Lester George Keen sat silent. Lester George Keen sat still on the edge of his motel bed, gazing at the blank walls around him. He could hear the white noise of TV static coming from the next room; just as though unpolished bustles could collapse. With bated breath, there was a cram smile on his face.

Lester George Keen sat silent on the edge of his motel bed, staring at the four hollow walls around him. Keen wanted to know what time it was, but his watch had stopped.

The simple grandeur of it all. The intensity of the immaterial involved. The motel, the room, the static, the stillness; the desert air. It was what he wanted most of all. It was the only thing you could do with an void.

There was only one thing you could do with an empty hole. To do nothing at all. He loved that most of all. Unrefined panicky digs set fires to medicine exaggerated cavities. Sly uy.

Without ego there can be no modesty. Humility is a byproduct of ego. The ego is a real indication that there's an understanding of how to transexpand a problem by possible inappropriateness.

Zreufaadinfied wadufadjads yaduyfadid the sydasiods and fadyesaked five asydesidsen veshads. An act of possible inappropriateness was Lester George Keen sitting silent on the edge of his motel bed. Manrissnakislekoodseeluwt had shackled duplicate semblances. Only to find shrinking sovhekjsion, uncertainty became xaatoogeekisisyding; as caverns den the hovel. Then too breaking elobosiveness beau.

Arrogance is the opposite of ego. Arrogance is a strong indication that there wont be any experiences beyond the palpable. With a complete lack of arrogance, Lester George Keen sat silent on his motel bed.

The air in his room was rotating around around him with the colour of weather in between the sand. Ewygawifjah-fihofeds fsoufosojohosagosa-nined the dosaiudosiuhosody ioudsojhodsioes.

The air in his room was rotating around him around him with the colour of weather in between the scent of sand. Shattering air rotated between him and the walls of this motel room. He could feel the torn pieces of air move about.

He could feel the torn pieces of air move around him in the room. It tickled a little. Shattering air.

Adventure on the High Seas

Shattering air rotated around him. Tickled a little. Small motel room. He was alone to feel the slivers of air rotate around him. He remained alone to feel the slivers of air rotate around him. And there was this scent of sand.

Ultra-low-frequency whistles were emitting out of his closet from the weight of his clothes sagging down on the wire hangers.

Large coloured tongues of paint were cracking and peeling slowly off the walls. He found this rot to be beautiful.

Large coloured tongues of paint were cracking and peeling slowly down off the walls. He found the texture of this sample of decay to be very beautiful. And slivers of air rotated around. The paint was faded on the walls. The paint was chipped.

BANG!!!

Once in a while the four walls would rise. Once in a while the four walls would lift up a little and separate.

Once in a while the four walls would lift a little and separate from the floor. Once in a while the four walls of his room would slowly lift up and separate from the floor. And after some seconds, slowly lower back down with the floor again.

When the walls would rise up and separate like this, they'd make a kind of clici-clic sound. A clici-clic twang.

Sparks fired out from the electric outlets, and he could hear empty TV static coming from behind the walls in the next room. He could hear this video static twitching and vibrating in the air around him. It tickled a bit.

A hole vibrating in a specific manner might be perceived as being a particular something.

The same hole folding and shaking in a particularly different manner may be perceived as being a specific something else. Both perceptions would be equally correct. An entity remains unchanged by the act of being seen.

Lester George Keen first came across his darling desert while scanning for a small horizon of mountain peaks.

He first came across his very favourite desert while in low orbit. Scanning for a small horizon of mountain peaks he heard about for some reason. What he found instead was a solitude expanding lay yonder the groves and minarets.

What expand did lay yonder! The groves and minarets of added adventure. Something of a gamble, maybe. POW!!!

Now he sat, still looking at those blank walls. Down the hall from his endearing room was an elevator. Its doors could be heard to randomly open and close all day long, all night long. Without the elevator itself ever moving up or down.

His mind was elsewhere. Fissure formed by breakage; clici-clic. He was thinking about stillness and anergy.

His mind thought about eternity and infinity as being unconnected. Eternity as a compilation of temporary occurrences. With infinity as the void located between the passing of events.

His body continued to sit still. His mind continued to think of slight separations outwards again.

And there he was; the blank walls were unaffected by his observation. Atoms occasioned independently of his thoughts. He was free to think of them any way he wanted. Everything is true regardless if it's false or not.

All judgments are equally incomplete unless combined with as many contradictions as possible. Frantic mangles kindled.

His mind was elsewhere; thinking about counting, about numbers, about blankness, about the desert outside. He was thinking of velocity and voidness, of the wind blowing grains of sand against his window. He thought of the desert outside.

He thought about the desert. Lester George Keen thought about subatomic particles bending and twitching. A flash twinkled ex officio.

Adventure on the High Seas

Bending and, bending and twitching out in the desert outside. When night came, stones out in the desert would explode. Twitch prickled, then burst rupture. The temperature at dusk would drop so quickly, rock broke. Bending and twitching out in the desert outside.

He thought about the desert. Lester George Keen thought about subatomic particles bending and twitching.

He would think about the desert, about similarities, about all things being a combination of location and direction. He was thinking of solids, liquids, and fluid gas. He thought of saliva and metal thrown about.

Sure, he had anticipations. Even a few regrets. Everybody had them. He just didn't think of such things. Unrestrained vacancy; waste exiled from release.

Eternity and infinity were two different things. He sat by the edge of his bed. What happened next didn't happen for some time, it happened immediately. He thought how things were only totally perfect when they were somewhat flawed.

In whatever he did, he would always keep in mind the inherent contradictions of biology.

Boiling up in a chilly hard smoke, the desert outside was freezing red hot. Eternity and infinity were two different things. Lester George Keen heard empty TV static coming from the next room; it was a good day and he felt fine.

His body was calm, but his mind was thinking thinking thinking. His intellect was both senseless and brutal. It was all very courageous.

"Tky" is an old word that means the samething as "serous". Tky is a unit of measurement. One tky is equal to logic as the predictability of emotion. What Lester George Keen was feeling could be summed up as serous.

Then for 32 days his mind went blank. He just didn't think about anything. Not a thing at all. Nada.

Later, an idea crashed softly through his mind. That rot and decay were the guiding principles of separateness and distance. The exception laid in between. He continued to sit on the edge of the bed, closely examining the blank walls.

Then his thoughts turned to wrestlers, elevators and anti-time. He studied not the walls, but their blankness. Raised trickles leap literally with a blow. Provoked accuracy was glorified while flare fatales blaze. Colloquial effervesce barked catchy pitches.

It was no different than the bareness of the desert outside. The naked hourglass still. Sand moving across from one bulb to the other. Separate differences identical to equivalent. CRASH!!! Interchangeable with any aberration.

It was no different than the bareness of the desert outside his room. Faultless blunders so unparalleled.

All his thoughts were now of wrestlers, elevators and anti-time. A skillful neglect regarding the bareness of the desert outside. Another faultless blunder. His intellect was both senseless and brutal. His body was calm, but his mind!

Then! For another five weeks, his mind went completely blank again. This time there were no thoughts of any kind.

The desert outside his motel laid in solitude, with total indifference to any thought anyone might have had about it. The wind breezed granules to wander. Sand screamed an inflated flatness ahoy; and powder gravelled a gale ashore.

Rough bises bellowed polished rock to sprinkle dust. On solid ground, sand dunes burst into throttled twists and turns.

The sandshore outside breezed ahoy a gale in solitude. Granules sprinkled tough twists and turns. Solid ground screamed bellowed polish. Shattering air rotated around the small motel. He was alone to feel the slivers of air rotate all around.

Adventure on the High Seas

Land ahoy with total indifference to the dunes gravelled with dust. Air slivers rotated around. Unrefined panicky digs set fires to medicine exaggerated cavities. Sly uy.

Wandering winds galed granules to breeze a rough powder bise. Once in a while his four walls would rise. Once in a while his four walls would lift up a little and separate from the floor. Once in a while the four walls of his room would slowly lift up.

When his four walls would rise and separate like this, they would make a kind of clici-clic twang of a bark.

Self-growth is meaning without rhyme or reason. Self-growth for him would be the ever changing sum of how many meanings he could give his preconceptions. Sat by the edge of the bed, counting all his implications over and over again. Manrissnakislekoodseeluwt had shackled duplicate semblances. Only to find shrinking sovhekjsion, uncertainty became xaatoogeekisisyding; as caverns den the hovel. Then too breaking elobosiveness beau.

The walls would be clici-clicing up and down, as he counted all his implications again and again.

Up and down. Clici-clic. Clici-clic. Down and up clici-clic. Clici-clic. Clici-clic down and down. Clici-clic. Clici-clic. Clici-clic up and up. Up and down. Up and down clici-clic; clici-clic; clici-clic... Clici-clic. Clici-clic. Up. Down. Insurgent welds seethed.

When his four walls would rise and separate like this, they would make a kind of clici-clic twang of a sound.

All his thoughts were of wrestlers, elevators and anti-time. Another faultless blunder. His intellect was so senseless and brutal. A skillful neglect regarding the bareness of the desert outside. His body was calm, but his mind!

Great herds of dust mites were stampeding across his bed. Lester George Keen was closely examining the blank.

Just outside the motel, granules of debris crumbled grittily. Diminutive abrasions sprinkled. Dust decreased detractions.

Furfuraceous fixed friabled filings to friction. Wee erosion abraded slippers to thong flip-flop the loafest.

Filings friabled to friction so wee erosion abraded slippers thong the flip-flop loafest. Naked queued dyed squats grubbed nearby.

Ambled notions flip-flopped in his thoughts. Despite all his social connections and associations, he still felt completely detached from everyone. From who they were, and from what they allured to. He had always felt this way. Even before birth he travelled.

Despite his connections and associations, he still felt completely detached from everyone.

Detached from who they were, and from what they allured at. He had always felt this way. Even before birth. So he travelled to meet his solitude face to face. Sure, solitude was a faceless traveller, but everyone still like to call him Sam.

Half way through a long flight between two distant planets, he met Sam. There he was, just looking right back at him. Meaty dwindles were ever faulty.

Lester George Keen was examining the blank, while Sam just looked right back at him. Sam was a resilient and devoted companion. Lester had reached out. And Sam was there for him. Dark red stars against that black sky. White stars flicked in from behind.

Dark red stars against that black of black sky. Kendeioeweks equfiogopeged feipagers of gepired giggurgurly geore-groges. White stars flicked in from behind. The air was warm with calm.

"Well fancy that then!" said Sam. Particles energized had begun jumping. As objects bounced around, gaps opened up beneath them. While hiding in their hole, the floor gave way. The next thing Lester George Keen saw were some immense thoughts looking right back at him.

Adventure on the High Seas

He didn't talk to any of the other motel guests. He just kept to himself. Thinking to himself. Again, this exceptional wreckage feathered ejaculation.

Thinking immense thoughts to himself. His last visit saw him walking about outside in the dunes. This latest visit saw him never leaving his room. Lester George Keen didn't talk to any of the other guests. He had no idea who they were.

Day after day, he sat on the edge of his bed; thinking, and looking blankly at the walls.

One day he thought of clepsammia as the stillness of time measured against the flow of sand. Measured against the flow of sand, he sat day after day on the edge of the bed. Looking at the blank walls, while Sam there just looked right back at him.

BANG!!!

Solitude was Lester George Keen's impermeable buffer that held all serious hazards at bay.

The sentinel that kept perils at bay. This was Sam. This was what was looking right back at him from the blankness of the four walls around him; strength through emptiness. Day after day, he sat on the edge of his bed; thinking... and thinking more.

And thinking more of subatomic particles bending and twitching. He thought about the desert.

Solitude, being the kind of sanctuary that it was, gave one the time needed for the contemplation of possibilities. Things occasionally fall apart quicker than one would like. Solitude gave one enough time for study.

Solitude gave one more than enough time to study the nature of something before one got far too committed. Miscellaneous flogging jiggles crystallized the evidence.

CRASH!!!

Things would occasionally fall apart quicker than one would like. Aloneness gave one enough time to study the nature of something before one got too involved. The only pitfall was that sometimes one could take too long to ponder.

Solitude was Lester George Keen's impermeable buffer that held all serious hazards at bay.

The sentinel that kept perils at bay. POW!!! This was Sam. This was what was looking right back at him from the blankness of the four walls around him; strength through emptiness. Day after day, he sat on the edge of his bed; thinking... and thinking more.

And thinking more of subatomic particles bending and twitching. He thought about the desert. Unrefined panicky digs set fires to medicine exaggerated cavities. Sly uy.

Solitude, being the kind of sanctuary that it was, gave one the time needed for the contemplation of possibilities. Things occasionally fall apart quicker than one would like. Solitude gave one enough time for study.

Solitude gave one more than enough time to study the nature of something before one got far too committed. Unrefined panicky digs set fires to medicine exaggerated cavities. Sly uy.

Things would occasionally fall apart quicker than one would like. Zoefiyogejofdufodbogodokods disfiwywjidibifikihouyjihed every wresarsycijohygiyn edridyudboofer and dehigeudugfuifnoobist on Zydiughonbohokhiujdogfosofia. Qurewtoofoodoofooboods were dydyhydidhudlly fakgohaaohjable!!! Aloneness gave one enough time to study the nature of something before one got too involved. The only pitfall was that sometimes one could take too long to ponder.

One could take too long to ponder. But this was the right moment for being where he was. He was thinking about the desert, and thinking of subatomic particles bending and twitching. He sat day after day on the edge of the bed. Looking at the blank walls, while solitude there smiled right back at him.

Adventure on the High Seas

The white noise hiss of the TV static coming from the next room was suddenly getting louder.

The hiss of the static coming from the next room was getting alot louder. He could feel a grain of sand squeezed in every pore of his skin. Herds of dust mites were stampeding across his bed. Lester George Keen was closely examining the blank.

People in the next room were watching blank static on a TV set while slowly cutting cardboard. Tainted alkaline glared.

Three people in the next room were staring into the blank static of a television set while slowly cutting up large pieces of cardboard with small knifes. Cutting very slowly. Sitting side-by-side in rocking chairs. Cutting very slowly.

People in the next room were watching blank static on a TV set while slowly cutting cardboard. Ewygawifjahfihofeds fsou-fosojohosagosa-nined the dosaiudosiuhosody ioudsojhodsioes.

Thinking immense thoughts. He didn't talk to any of the other guests. He just kept to himself. Thinking to himself immense thoughts. His last visit saw him walking about in the dunes. This latest visit saw him never leaving his motel room. Obsessive needs too grab austerity.

Lester George Keen didn't talk to any of the other guests. He had no idea who any of them were. Unrefined panicky digs set fires to medicine exaggerated cavities. Sly uy.

He had no idea who any of these other guests were. Day after day, he sat on the edge of his bed; thinking, and looking blankly at the walls. One day he thought of clepsammia as the stillness of time measured against the flow of sand.

Measured against the flow of sand, he sat day after day on the edge of the bed. Looking at the blank walls.

Another day found him thinking about the disembodied voices he's heard on the radio; of shovels in the ground, and fireballs in the sky. He didn't talk to none of the other guests. He just kept to himself. Thinking for himself.

Thinking, thinking, thinking. Before birth, his thinking dealt with randomly picking what preconceptions to have. Zodiacally, zealous blanks zip honest! Unrefined panicky digs set fires to medicine exaggerated cavities. Sly uy.

Before birth, all his thought dealt with randomly picking what preconceptions to have. After birth, his thinking dealt with finding excuses to back up his preconceptions. Measuring the assumption with the excuse would end up being his plan. Unrefined panicky digs set fires to medicine exaggerated cavities. Sly uy.

Measuring the assumption to the excuse would end up being his attempt to evacuate all evidence of his existence from the environment, and gain peace of mind. Just no better place, he thought, than to do this at a desert.

Best place for this, he thought, was a desert. Luckily for his mind, his body always ended up near one. Unrefined panicky digs set fires to medicine exaggerated cavities. Sly uy.

Regret didn't enter into any of this. Lester George Keen just didn't give any attention to such things. What he was doing at this motel and at this desert was just another element of the chaos of biology.

With the chaos of biology, he would have done it by chance, regardless if he had done it, or not.

By chance he would soon be travelling by sitting still on the edge of his bed. By chance he would soon be travelling by sitting still in his room. And not just because the motel was being carried off to somewhere else by a spinning planet.

Because his mind was spinning between his body and the void nothingness. He sat looking at the blank walls.

There was something else he thought about. With biology dependent on unstable molecules to modulate energy between the stable ones, rot and decay become the balance of weak and strong. This was irony. This was, well; funny.

He then thought about how many light-years in flight he'd accumulated with all the space-travel he'd done.

Lester George Keen sat silent. Lester George Keen sat still on the edge of his motel bed, gazing at the blank walls around him. He could hear the white noise of TV static coming from the next room. With bated breath, there was a cram smile on his face.

Lester George Keen sat silent on the edge of his motel bed, staring at the four hollow walls around him.

The simple grandeur of it all. The intensity of the immaterial involved. The motel, the room, the static, the stillness; the desert air. It was what he wanted most of all. It was the only thing you could do with an void.

There was only one thing you could do with an empty hole. To do nothing at all. He loved that most of all.

Without ego there can be no modesty. Humility is a by-product of ego. The ego is a real indication that there's an understanding of how to transexpand a problem by possible inappropriateness.

An act of possible inappropriateness was Lester George Keen sitting silent on the edge of his motel bed.

Arrogance is the opposite of ego. Arrogance is a strong indication that there wont be any experiences beyond the palpable. With a complete lack of arrogance, Lester George Keen sat silent on his motel bed.

The air in his room was rotating around around him with the colour of weather in between the sand.

The air in his room was rotating around him around him with the colour of weather in between the scent of sand. Shattering air rotated between him and the walls of this motel room. He could feel the torn pieces of air move about.

He could feel the torn pieces of air move around him in the room. It tickled a little. Kendeioeweks equfiogopeged feipagers of gepired giggurgurly geore-groges. Shattering air.

Shattering air rotated around him. Tickled a little. Small motel room. He was alone to feel the slivers of air rotate around him. He remained alone to feel the slivers of air rotate around him. And there was this scent of sand.

Large coloured tongues of paint were cracking and peeling slowly off the walls. He found this rot to be beautiful.

Large coloured tongues of paint were cracking and peeling slowly down off the walls. He found the texture of this sample of decay to be very beautiful. And slivers of air rotated around. The paint was faded on the walls. The paint was chipped.

Once in a while the four walls would rise. Once in a while the four walls would lift up a little and separate.

Once in a while the four walls would lift a little and separate from the floor. Once in a while the four walls of his room would slowly lift up and separate from the floor. And after some seconds, slowly lower back down with the floor again.

When the walls would rise up and separate like this, they'd make a kind of clici-clic sound. A clici-clic twang.

Sparks fired out from the electric outlets, and he could hear empty TV static coming from behind the walls in the next room. He could hear this video static twitching and vibrating in the air around him. It tickled a bit.

A hole vibrating in a specific manner might be perceived as being a particular something.

The same hole folding and shaking in a particularly different manner may be perceived as being a specific something else. Both perceptions would be equally correct. An entity remains unchanged by the act of being seen.

Zreufaadinfied wadufadjads yaduyfadid the sydasiods and fadyesaked five asydesidsen veshads. Lester George Keen first came across his darling desert while scanning for a small horizon of mountain peaks.

He first came across his very favourite desert while in low orbit. Scanning for a small horizon of mountain peaks he heard about for some reason. What he found instead was a solitude expanding lay yonder the groves and minarets.

What expand did lay yonder! BANG!!! The groves and minarets of added adventure. Something of a gamble, maybe. Manrissnakislekoodseeluwt had shackled duplicate semblances. Only to find shrinking sovhekjsion, uncertainty became xaatoogeekisisyding; as caverns den the hovel. Then too breaking elobosiveness beau.

Now he sat, still looking at those blank walls. Down the hall from his endearing room was an elevator. Its doors could be heard to randomly open and close all day long, all night long. Without the elevator itself ever moving up or down.

His mind was elsewhere. Fissure formed by breakage; clici-clic. He was thinking about stillness and anergy.

His mind thought about eternity and infinity as being unconnected. Eternity as a compilation of temporary occurrences. With infinity as the void located between the passing of events.

His body continued to sit still. His mind continued to think of slight separations outwards again.

And there he was; the blank walls were unaffected by his observation. Atoms occasioned independently of his thoughts. He was free to think of them any way he wanted. Everything is true regardless if it's false or not.

All judgments are equally incomplete unless combined with as many contradictions as possible.

His mind was elsewhere; thinking about counting, about numbers, about blankness, about the desert outside. He was thinking of velocity and voidness, of the wind blowing grains of sand against his window. He thought of the desert outside.

He thought about the desert. Lester George Keen thought about subatomic particles bending and twitching.

Bending and, bending and twitching out in the desert outside. When night came, stones out in the desert would explode. Twitch prickled, then burst rupture. The temperature at dusk would drop so quickly, rock broke. Bending and twitching out in the desert outside.

He thought about the desert. Lester George Keen thought about subatomic particles bending and twitching.

He would think about the desert, about similarities, about all things being a combination of location and direction. He was thinking of solids, liquids, and fluid gas. He thought of saliva and metal thrown about.

Sure, he had anticipations. Even a few regrets. Everybody had them. He just didn't think of such things.

Eternity and infinity were two different things. He sat by the edge of his bed. What happened next didn't happen for some time, it happened immediately. He thought how things were only totally perfect when they were somewhat flawed.

In whatever he did, he would always keep in mind the inherent contradictions of biology.

Boiling up in a chilly hard smoke, the desert outside was freezing red hot. Eternity and infinity were two different things. Lester George Keen heard empty TV static coming from the next room; it was a good day and he felt fine.

His body was calm, but his mind was thinking thinking thinking. His intellect was both senseless and brutal.

"Tky" is an old word that means the samething as "serous". Tky is a unit of measurement. One tky is equal to logic as the predictability of emotion. What Lester George Keen was feeling could be summed up as serous.

Adventure on the High Seas

Then for 32 days his mind went blank. He just didn't think about anything. Not a thing at all. Nada.

POW!!!

Later, an idea crashed softly through his mind. That rot and decay were the guiding principles of separateness and distance. The exception laid in between. He continued to sit on the edge of the bed, closely examining the blank walls.

Then his thoughts turned to wrestlers, elevators and anti-time. He studied not the walls, but their blankness.

It was no different than the bareness of the desert outside. The naked hourglass still. Sand moving across from one bulb to the other. Separate differences identical to equivalent. Interchangeable with any aberration.

It was no different than the bareness of the desert outside his room. Faultless blunders so unparalleled.

All his thoughts were now of wrestlers, elevators and anti-time. A skillful neglect regarding the bareness of the desert outside. Another faultless blunder. His intellect was both senseless and brutal. His body was calm, but his mind!

Then! For another five weeks, his mind went completely blank again. This time there were no thoughts of any kind.

The desert outside his motel laid in solitude, with total indifference to any thought anyone might have had about it. The wind breezed granules to wander. Sand screamed an inflated flatness ahoy; and powder gravelled a gale ashore.

Rough bises bellowed polished rock to sprinkle dust. On solid ground, sand dunes burst into throttled twists and turns.

The sandshore outside breezed ahoy a gale in solitude. Granules sprinkled tough twists and turns. Solid ground screamed bellowed polish. Shattering air rotated around the small motel. He was alone to feel the slivers of air rotate all around.

Land ahoy with total indifference to the dunes gravelled with dust. Air slivers rotated around.

Wandering winds galed granules to breeze a rough powder bise. Once in a while his four walls would rise. Once in a while his four walls would lift up a little and separate from the floor. Once in a while the four walls of his room would slowly lift up.

When his four walls would rise and separate like this, they would make a kind of clici-clic twang of a bark.

Self-growth is meaning without rhyme or reason. Self-growth for him would be the ever changing sum of how many meanings he could give his preconceptions. Sat by the edge of the bed, counting all his implications over and over again.

Great herds of dust mites were stampeding across his bed. Lester George Keen was closely examining the blank.

Just outside the motel, granules of debris crumbled grittily. Diminutive abrasions sprinkled. Dust decreased detractions. Furfuraceous fixed friabled filings to friction. BANG!!! Wee erosion abraded slippers to thong flip-flop the loafest.

Filings friabled to friction so wee erosion abraded slippers thong the flip-flop loafest.

Ambled notions flip-flopped in his thoughts. Despite all his social connections and associations, he still felt completely detached from everyone. From who they were, and from what they allured to. He had always felt this way. Even before birth he travelled.

Despite his connections and associations, he still felt completely detached from everyone.

Detached from who they were, and from what they allured at. He had always felt this way. Even before birth. So he travelled to meet his solitude face to face. Sure, solitude was a faceless traveller, but everyone still like to call him Sam.

Half way through a long flight between two distant planets, he met Sam. There he was, just looking right back at him.

Adventure on the High Seas

Lester George Keen was examining the blank, while Sam just looked right back at him. Sam was a resilient and devoted companion. Lester had reached out. And Sam was there for him. Dark red stars against that black sky. White stars flicked in from behind.

Dark red stars against that black of black sky. White stars flicked in from behind. The air was warm with calm.

"Well fancy that then!" said Sam. Particles energized had begun jumping. As objects bounced around, gaps opened up beneath them. While hiding in their hole, the floor gave way. The next thing Lester George Keen saw were some immense thoughts looking right back at him.

He didn't talk to any of the other motel guests. He just kept to himself. Thinking to himself.

Thinking immense thoughts to himself. His last visit saw him walking about outside in the dunes. This latest visit saw him never leaving his room. Lester George Keen didn't talk to any of the other guests. He had no idea who they were.

Day after day, he sat on the edge of his bed; thinking, and looking blankly at the walls. Ultra-low-frequency whistles were emitting out of his closet from the weight of his clothes sagging down on the wire hangers.

One day he thought of clepsammia as the stillness of time measured against the flow of sand. Measured against the flow of sand, he sat day after day on the edge of the bed. Looking at the blank walls, while Sam there just looked right back at him.

Solitude was Lester George Keen's impermeable buffer that held all serious hazards at bay.

The sentinel that kept perils at bay. This was Sam. This was what was looking right back at him from the blankness of the four walls around him; strength through emptiness. Day after day, he sat on the edge of his bed; thinking... and thinking more.

And thinking more of subatomic particles bending and twitching. He thought about the desert.

Solitude, being the kind of sanctuary that it was, gave one the time needed for the contemplation of possibilities. Things occasionally fall apart quicker than one would like. Solitude gave one enough time for study.

Solitude gave one more than enough time to study the nature of something before one got far too committed.

Things would occasionally fall apart quicker than one would like. Aloneness gave one enough time to study the nature of something before one got too involved. The only pitfall was that sometimes one could take too long to ponder.

Solitude gave one more than enough time to study the nature of something before one got far too committed.

One could take too long to ponder. But this was the right moment for being where he was. He was thinking about the desert, and thinking of subatomic particles bending and twitching. He sat day after day on the edge of the bed. Looking at the blank walls, while solitude there smiled right back at him.

BANG!!!

Nada. Not a thing at all. He just didn't think about anything. Then for 32 days his mind went blank.

He thought about the desert. Lester George Keen thought about subatomic particles bending and twitching. When night came, stones out in the desert would explode. The temperature at dusk would drop so quickly that rock broke. Out in the desert outside.

He thought about the desert. Lester George Keen thought about subatomic particles bending and twitching.

What Lester George Keen was feeling could be summed up as serous. Tky is a unit of measurement. One tky is equal to logic as the predictability of emotion. "Tky" is an old word that means the samething as "serous".

Adventure on the High Seas

CRASH!!!

His intellect was both senseless and brutal. His body was calm, but his mind was thinking thinking thinking.

Lester George Keen heard empty TV static coming from the next room; it was a good day and he felt fine. Eternity and infinity were two different things. Boiling up in a chilly hard smoke, the desert outside was freezing red hot.

In whatever he did, he would always keep in mind the inherent contradictions of biology.

He thought how things were only totally perfect when they were somewhat flawed. What happened next didn't happen for some time, it happened immediately. He sat by the edge of his bed. Eternity and infinity were two different things.

He just didn't think of such things. Everybody had them. Even a few regrets. Sure, he had anticipations.

He thought of saliva and metal thrown about. He was thinking of solids, liquids, and fluid gas. He would think about the desert, about similarities, about all things being a combination of location and direction.

He thought about the desert. Lester George Keen thought about subatomic particles bending and twitching.

He thought of the desert outside. He was thinking of velocity and voidness, of the wind blowing grains of sand against his window. His mind was elsewhere; thinking about counting, about numbers, about blankness, about the desert outside.

All judgments are equally incomplete unless combined with as many contradictions as possible.

POW!!!

Everything is true regardless if it's false or not. He was free to think of them any way he wanted. Atoms occasioned independently of his thoughts. And there he was; the blank walls were unaffected by his observation.

His mind continued to think of slight separations outwards again. His body continued to sit still.

With infinity as the void located between the passing of events. Eternity as a compilation of temporary occurrences. His mind thought about eternity and infinity as being unconnected.

He was thinking about stillness and anergy. Fissure formed by breakage; clici-clic. His mind was elsewhere.

Without the elevator itself ever moving up or down. Its doors could be heard to randomly open and close all day long, all night long. Down the hall from his endearing room was an elevator. Now he sat, still looking at those blank walls.

Something of a gamble, maybe. The groves and minarets of added adventure. What expand did lay yonder!

What he found instead was a solitude expanding lay yonder the groves and minarets. Scanning for a small horizon of mountain peaks he heard about for some reason. He first came across his very favourite desert while in low orbit.

Lester George Keen first came across his darling desert while scanning for a small horizon of mountain peaks.

An entity remains unchanged by the act of being seen. Infinitely acquires insignificance through argue combination deserted. Nothingness done articulated in regard to. Zilch as far as absolute about else.

A hole vibrating in a specific manner might be perceived as being a particular something. Zoefiyogejofdufodbogodokods disfiwywjidibifikihouyjihed every wresarsycijohygiyn edridyud-boofer and dehigeudugfuifnoobist on Zydiughonbohokhiujdog-fosofia. Qurewtoofoodoofooboods were dydyhydidhudlly fakgo-haaohjable!!!

It tickled a bit. He could hear this video static twitching and vibrating in the air around him. Sparks fired out from the electric outlets, and he could hear empty TV static coming from behind the walls in the next room.

Adventure on the High Seas

A clici-clic twang. When the walls would rise up and separate like this, they'd make a kind of clici-clic sound. Kendeioeweks equfiogopeged feipagers of gepired giggurgurly geore-groges.

And after some seconds, slowly lower back down with the floor again. Once in a while the four walls of his room would slowly lift up and separate from the floor. Once in a while the four walls would lift a little and separate from the floor.

Once in a while the four walls would lift up a little and separate. Ewygawifjahfihofeds fsoufosojohosagosa-nined the dosaiudosiuhosody ioudsojhodsioes. Once in a while the four walls would rise.

The paint was chipped. The paint was faded on the walls. And slivers of air rotated around. He found the texture of this sample of decay to be very beautiful. Large coloured tongues of paint were cracking and peeling slowly down off the walls.

He found this rot to be beautiful. Large coloured tongues of paint were cracking and peeling slowly off the walls.

Zreufaadinfied wadufadjads yaduyfadid the sydasiods and fadyesaked five asydesidsen veshads. And there was this scent of sand. He remained alone to feel the slivers of air rotate around him. He was alone to feel the slivers of air rotate around him. Small motel room. Tickled a little. Shattering air rotated around him.

Shattering air. It tickled a little. He could feel the torn pieces of air move around him in the room. Manrissnakislekoodsee-luwt had shackled duplicate semblances. Only to find shrinking sovhekjsion, uncertainty became xaatoogeekisisyding; as caverns den the hovel. Then too breaking elobosiveness beau.

He could feel the torn pieces of air move about. Shattering air rotated between him and the walls of this motel room. The air in his room was rotating around him around him with the colour of weather in between the scent of sand.

The air in his room was rotating around around him with the colour of weather in between the sand.

With a complete lack of arrogance, Lester George Keen sat silent on his motel bed. Arrogance is a strong indication that there wont be any experiences beyond the palpable. Arrogance is the opposite of ego.

An act of possible inappropriateness was Lester George Keen sitting silent on the edge of his motel bed.

The ego is a real indication that there's an understanding of how to transexpand a problem by possible inappropriateness. Humility is a byproduct of ego. Without ego there can be no modesty.

To do nothing at all. He loved that most of all. There was only one thing you could do with an empty hole.

It was the only thing you could do with an void. It was what he wanted most of all. The motel, the room, the static, the stillness; the desert air. The intensity of the immaterial involved. The simple grandeur of it all.

Lester George Keen sat silent on the edge of his motel bed, staring at the four hollow walls around him.

With bated breath, there was a cram smile on his face. He could hear the white noise of TV static coming from the next room. Lester George Keen sat still on the edge of his motel bed, gazing at the blank walls around him. Lester George Keen sat silent.

He then thought about how many light-years in flight he'd accumulated with all the space-travel he'd done.

This was, well; funny. This was irony. With biology dependent on unstable molecules to modulate energy between the stable ones, rot and decay become the balance of weak and strong. There was something else he thought about.

He sat looking at the blank walls. Because his mind was spinning between his body and the void nothingness.

Adventure on the High Seas

And not just because the motel was being carried off to somewhere else by a spinning planet. By chance he would soon be travelling by sitting still in his room. Ewygawifjahfihofeds fsoufosojohosagosa-nined the dosaiudosiuhosody ioudsojhodsioes. By chance he would soon be travelling by sitting still on the edge of his bed.

With the chaos of biology, he would have done it by chance, regardless if he had done it, or not. Ewygawifjahfihofeds fsoufosojohosagosa-nined the dosaiudosiuhosody ioudsojhodsioes.

What he was doing at this motel and at this desert was just another element of the chaos of biology. Lester George Keen just didn't give any attention to such things. Regret didn't enter into any of this.

Luckily for his mind, his body always ended up near one. Best place for this, he thought, was a desert.

Just no better place, he thought, than to do this at a desert. Measuring the assumption to the excuse would end up being his attempt to evacuate all evidence of his existence from the environment, and gain peace of mind. Zoefiyogejofdufodbogodokods disfiwywjidibifikihouyjihed every wresarsycijohygiyn edridyudboofer and dehigeudugfuifnoobist on Zydiughonbohokhiujdogfosofia. Qurewtoofoodoofooboods were dydyhydidhudlly fakgohaaohjable!!!

Measuring the assumption with the excuse would end up being his plan. After birth, his thinking dealt with finding excuses to back up his preconceptions. Before birth, all his thought dealt with randomly picking what preconceptions to have.

Before birth, his thinking dealt with randomly picking what preconceptions to have. Ewygawifjahfihofeds fsoufosojohosagosa-nined the dosaiudosiuhosody ioudsojhodsioes. Thinking, thinking, thinking.

Thinking for himself. He just kept to himself. He didn't talk to none of the other guests. Another day found him thinking about the disembodied voices he's heard on the radio; of shovels in the ground, and fireballs in the sky.

Looking at the blank walls. Measured against the flow of sand, he sat day after day on the edge of the bed.

One day he thought of clepsammia as the stillness of time measured against the flow of sand. Day after day, he sat on the edge of his bed; thinking, and looking blankly at the walls. He had no idea who any of these other guests were.

He had no idea who any of them were. Lester George Keen didn't talk to any of the other guests.

This latest visit saw him never leaving his motel room. His last visit saw him walking about in the dunes. Thinking to himself immense thoughts. He just kept to himself. He didn't talk to any of the other guests. Thinking immense thoughts.

This latest visit saw him never leaving his room. His last visit saw him walking about in the sands.

Thinking immense thoughts. This most recent hiatus saw him never leaving his room. The wind blew so hard, it blasted a grain of sand into every pore of his skin. The air was hot and dry. His last visit saw him walking around in the dunes.

This latest visit saw him never leaving his room. His last visit saw him walking about in the sands.

Thoughts immense thinking, room motel his in staying him saw visit latest this. Sand of bits counting dunes the through. Dunes the through wandering aimlessly him saw visit last his. Desert this loved he. Again time and time made had he trip a was it.

Planet another from way the all travelled Keen George Laster. Wide and far all from came motel this at quests the.

Desert this loved he. Again time and time made had he trip a was it. Planet another from way the all travelled Keen George

Adventure on the High Seas

Lester one; motel this at staying were guests several. Desert vast an of edge thin the on motel only the was it.

Remote this at staying were quests several and desert vast an of edge the on motel only the was it.

Thoughts immense thinking, room motel his in staying him saw visit latest this. Sand of bits counting dunes the through. Dunes the through wandering aimlessly him saw visit last his. Desert this loved he. Again time and time made had he trip a was it.

Corrosion would broadside erosion. Crumbly grit flecked speckwards. Crumbly grit cropping idlers everywhere. Manriss-nakislekoodseeluwt had shackled duplicate semblances. Only to find shrinking sovhekjsion, uncertainty became xaatoogee-kisisyding; as caverns den the hovel. Then too breaking elobosiveness beau.

What's your soul, but the substance of the time and place you find yourself. There's a void on either side, and another one in between. In between what? What's your soul? Lester George Keen was examining the blank, the inexhaustible blank, while outside fixations of fragments placed.

Lester George Keen was examining the blank, while outside fixations of fragments placed placement's shades.

Scraps severed the importance of his epic. Lester George Keen was examining the blank, and the blankness started to speak to him; "Frist you have intention, then meaning, followed by the word, and then debate. And the whole process is fueled by doubt."

Lester George Keen was examining the blank, while outside fixations of fragments placed placement's shades.

While examining the blank, Lester George Keen turned to notice how the sole light bulb in his room had remained intact, even after being pierced by a big furry moth. The moth vanished into the gentle radiance while outside bents place shades.

GX Jupitter-Larsen

Lester George Keen was examining the blank, while outside fixations of fragments placed placement's shades.

Lester George Keen was examining the blank, while outside fixations of fragments placed shades of placements post stand. Another ample dash was spanking its own magnitude. Profound scraps severed the importance of his own diminutive epic.

Not every moment counts. Only the accumulative effect of all the moments enumerates to anything. He just sat in his room, looking at the blank walls till he died. It was a triumphant death!

Then, dazzling polywaves wrapped around numerous searing ramshackles, chattering any push against existence. Bypassing all those numerous heavens and hells he could have chosen from, he found his own way by happily continuing on his narrative. He was a calm smile in life. So he would be a calm smile in death. It was a triumphant death.

The proto-philosopher slug, as if by pure instinct, dreamed of a mind that could think real thoughts. What did astronomers look at before there were any stars? The future is the wreckage of history, and the present is just the sound of everything falling apart! Conspicuous crumbling.

The Adventure Probabilities:

It seems that with every novel I smash together I encounter imposing visions in between the vomited vocabulary. Some are personally meaningful. These were incorporated into the novel. A few remain hopeful that chaos will find for them substance. In no particular order:

An astronomer in the southwest, during his 14th Kettleday, will have tried in every way to bring about reforms. Without success. As a consequence, a change takes place that will lead to an extraordinary embellishment. One so different from either nourishment or stabilization that criminal slithers escape danger.

While on his way home, during his 6th Kettleday, someone will prevent the cracking of acquired directions. Investigating a collection of fundamental fragments, the question of melancholy ambushes the larger penetration.

During a 32nd Kettleday, the relationship between unseen and decisive equilibrium stands bestowed. The aristocracy will then avoid rigid intent for undulating inclinations. And a suppression of support will yield a tolerance.

During a 21st Kettleday, empty restraints will be accumulated insistently in the middle-east. Controlling powers will be mindful of simultaneous tides of influence. A gathering together of dissolving elements will force difficulties sought out by a blue-haired attention.